Hunter's Moon

The DOCTOR WHO series from BBC Books

DOCTOR WHO

Hunter's Moon

PAUL FINCH

3 5 7 9 10 8 6 4

Published in 2011 by BBC Books, an imprint of Ebury Publishing
A Random House Group Company

Copyright © Paul Finch 2011

Paul Finch has asserted his right to be identified as the author of this Work in
accordance with the Copyright, Designs and Patents Act 1988.

Doctor Who is a BBC Wales production for BBC One.
Executive producers: Steven Moffat, Piers Wenger and Beth Willis
BBC, DOCTOR WHO and TARDIS (word marks, logos and devices) are
trademarks of the British Broadcasting Corporation and are used under licence.

The Random House Group Limited Reg. No. 954009
Addresses for companies within the Random House Group can be found
at www.randomhouse.co.uk
A CIP catalogue for this book is available from the British Library.

ISBN 978 1 849 90567 1

The Random House Group Limited supports The Forest Stewardship
Council® (FSC®), the leading international forest-certification organisation.
Our books carrying the FSC label are printed on FSC®-certified paper.
FSC is the only forest-certification scheme supported by the leading
environmental organisations, including Greenpeace. Our
paper procurement policy can be found at
www.randomhouse.co.uk/environment

MIX
Paper from
responsible sources
FSC® C016897

Commissioning editor: Albert DePetrillo
Editorial manager: Nicholas Payne
Series consultant: Justin Richards
Project editor: Steve Tribe
Cover design: Lee Binding © Woodlands Books Ltd 2011
Production: Rebecca Jones

Printed and bound in Great Britain by Clays Ltd, St Ives PLC

To buy books by your favourite authors and register for offers,
visit www.randomhouse.co.uk

Mallik ran as he'd never run before. He was young and strong, and though he had been running for hours already he knew that he could keep going for a while yet. This didn't mean that he wasn't aching all over, that his throat wasn't raw with gasping and panting. The air was foul in this place. It tasted bad, it smelled bad – it was filled with pollutants. But still Mallik ran, sucking it in in great lungfuls. He was staggering along a corrugated steel conduit. As if such a surface wasn't difficult enough, it was streaked with oil and grease, and strewn with a rubble of broken machine parts. And of course it was dark. It was always dark here.

Inevitably, he stumbled and fell.

He landed face-first. A jagged edge tore his chin and lower lip, the pain lancing through him. The metallic taste of blood filled his mouth. He spat it out as he hauled himself to his feet. His wheezing for breath was so loud that he imagined it could be heard for hundreds of metres along the conduit.

Not that it needed to be, because now, when he listened, he heard a *clank-clank* of approaching feet. He turned sharply. Around the corner, some twenty metres away, a figure appeared. It was indistinguishable in the dimness – apart from its eyes, from which two red laser beams blazed. They swept from one side of the passage to the next, quickly pin-pointing him. Mallik shrieked and threw himself to the ground. There was an ear-shattering *CRUMP* as an energy bolt struck the conduit wall close to where he'd been standing, showering him with red-hot shards.

Though dizzied by pain and concussion, Mallik wormed his way out through the smoking aperture. There was a drop on the other side, which for all he knew might plummet hundreds of metres onto more piles of scrap or into a corrosive sludge of waste-chemicals. But in fact he fell no more than a metre, landing on a rickety steel catwalk, which shuddered as he stumbled along it. A ladder appeared to his left. He climbed down it, staring back up towards the punctured conduit. That tall figure was in the process of clambering out. It wore bulky coveralls, tiger-striped black and grey, and an open-faced helmet with a black visor across the eyes. Below that, an oxygen mask was clamped to its nose and mouth, a rubber pipe snaking back over the shoulder, joining a tank-type assembly on its back. Another of the most futuristic rifles Mallik had ever seen was angled back across the figure's shoulder as it moved to the edge of the catwalk and gazed down, that burning laser vision spearing through the shadows.

Mallik reached the ground, and went full pelt towards the nearest wall. This was about five metres tall, though a portion of it had been smashed down when an overhead girder had rotted from its moorings. Mallik scrambled through and then was tumbling down a slope of bricks and smashed masonry. Somewhere to his left there was a towering skeletal structure. Was it his imagination or was another figure perched on one of its high parapets, taking aim at him? A green spark answered the question. He knew what that weapon was. They'd referred to it as 'the Eradicator'.

Even over this distance – there must have been fifty metres between the two of them – Mallik heard the rising hum as the energy pack charged itself, and with a whiplash *CRACK*, a great zigzag of electricity sizzled towards him. His heels shot forward and he landed hard on his back. The bolt slashed through the air only inches over his head, striking the impacted rubble. The blast threw Mallik to the bottom of the slope, where he lay helpless. His exhaustion now gave way to a terrible despair. He could sense that his back was damaged. When he tried to get to his feet, pain chewed through his spine like a buzz-saw.

With a clatter of bricks, the figure in stripes descended the slope towards him. From the other direction, the man with the Eradicator was climbing from his perch.

'No…' Mallik said under his breath. No… it wasn't going to end like this.

He dragged his broken body back up, and tried to run, though now it was more a comical caper. Blood filled his mouth, sweat blinded him. Another mountain of rubble rose directly in front, but there had to be a way round it. And indeed a path meandered off to his right along a ravine. He blundered along it, but he'd covered no more than twenty metres before the slope erupted beneath his feet in a welter of mud and foulness.

The octopoid horror that engulfed Mallik was not the worst thing he'd seen since coming here, but he couldn't imagine anything more terrible than the demise that suddenly faced him. The monster's thick, rubbery tentacles wrapped around him with bone-crushing force, their circular sucker pads oozing a sticky pus, which was soon slathered all over him, gluing his arms to his sides, his hair to his scalp, even gluing his wounded lips shut. With a gargling roar, and a stench like a vomit-filled dustbin, its maw gaped, revealing teeth that were slivers of curved, needle-tipped bone.

There was an ear-splitting *CRACK* as the Eradicator man spoke again.

Lightning struck the octo-horror clean in the mouth. There was a searing flash and a hideous stink of melting flesh.

Mallik was tossed to the ground, as the beast wailed in nightmarish agony.

Its ruptured bulk, still half-buried in the rubble, quivered and smoked, black ichor bursting from numerous orifices. Its limbs writhed and thrashed for minutes on end. Only when its cries subsided to a dull mewling, and its movements ceased, did the Eradicator man and the man in stripes feel it safe to approach.

Eradicator man chuckled. He was a compact fellow, whose lack of helmet revealed a badly scarred face and white hair shaven to bristles on top of his broad, flattish skull. His body was squat and powerful, encased in fatigues made from jet-black vinyl and hung over the shoulders with a short cape of greasy, matted fur. He shouldered his primary weapon, and drew a heavy pistol. Taking aim from point-blank range, he fired two deafening rounds into the creature. Gigantic shells tore holes the size of dinner plates in its blistered hide. There was no further sound from it. Two of its smouldering tentacles twitched feebly, and lay still.

Mallik could rise no further than his knees. His body was mangled, his bones multiply fractured. He was coated in gore and filth. Through his fading eyes, he saw bulkily clad figures trudging along the ravine.

Eradicator man glanced at the man in stripes, who had removed his oxygen mask, to reveal a cruelly grinning mouth. 'This last one's mine, I think?' Eradicator man said.

Stripes nodded.

Eradicator man placed the muzzle of his pistol to Mallik's head. 'Be honest,' he chuckled, 'you wouldn't want to live in your condition.'

Mallik stuttered: 'I... never thought I'd... I'd die... in a place like this.'

Eradicator man shrugged. '*We* like it. But as you Earth people say... home is where the heart is.'

He fired.

Chapter
1

Harry Mossop was aware that he exercised almost no control in his own home. But he was aware of a great many things that now seemed beyond his capability to fix – his employment situation, for example. After two decades as a police officer in the Met, earning decent money and enjoying all the respect and perks such a position had brought him, to suddenly find himself on the pittance that was Jobseeker's Allowance and whiling away tedious hours alternating between the mind-numbing distractions of daytime TV and the increasingly disheartening process of trying to find suitable work had been a culture shock of the first order.

Of course, things might have been easier had he had a police pension to draw on, and a glowing reference from his former employers in his pocket. But as he had neither of these, even two years on he still felt more unprepared for the rigours of ordinary civilian life than he could ever have imagined possible. It was his own fault – he was well aware of that, but a man could only go on berating himself for so long before self-pity replaced any stoic acknowledgement that he was getting what he deserved.

It was a dark, cold November evening when Dora returned from work looking as tired as usual. 'I'm here,' she said from the hall, in a tone which seemed to imply that arriving home from the supermarket was only marginally less depressing than arriving *at* the supermarket first thing in the morning.

Harry came down from the spare bedroom, where their computer was set up. As usual, he'd become so preoccupied with job-hunting that he hadn't done any household chores.

Dora sighed, as she dumped her bags. She tried to ignore the mass of laundry on the sofa, which he'd been supposed to iron, or the various items of Sophie's make-up which, as always, were arrayed along the mantelpiece. Dora ventured into the kitchen, where, with an expression of abject defeat, she viewed the pile of dirty crockery in the sink, some of which had been there so long that the food remnants on it had caked into a hard rind.

'I'll sort this out,' Harry said, coming in behind her. 'Don't worry.'

'It's all right, I'm here now.' She began sliding items into the dishwasher without even taking her coat off. 'Any sign of Sophie?'

'Nope,' he replied.

'Where is she?'

'Wouldn't know.'

Sophie – or rather, how to deal with Sophie – was another bone of contention between them. Their daughter was now 18, and they saw so little of her that she might as well be living away. As things were that suited Harry, even though Sophie would almost certainly be with Baz, her latest 'lounge lizard' boyfriend, who, like all the others before him, had no car, no money and no job (not that Harry could make too much of an issue of the latter flaw, as Sophie had several times reminded him). She was a dissatisfying daughter in so many ways, but Harry and Dora differed radically in their views on how to deal with her and, as this had led to several fiery confrontations, Harry was now always glad when the source of the friction was out of sight and out of mind.

'I wondered if you fancied popping out for a bite to eat tonight?' he said.

'Why… Something to celebrate?' Dora probably didn't mean it to sound quite so contemptuous.

'No, but anything to lighten the gloom.'

'That would really lighten the gloom, that would, Harry. Spending money we haven't got. We can't carry on like this. I'll just have to put in for more overtime.'

Harry shoved his hands into his pockets, and waited a couple of minutes before saying: 'I was thinking of going back to see Grant Pangborne.'

Dora turned and faced him. 'Why?'

Harry shrugged. 'As far as I know, he's still got a vacancy for a security officer.'

'Maybe, but if he isn't prepared to pay…?'

'Well, he's had a couple of months with no one on site. It's not too far off Christmas – lots of burglaries at this time of year. Maybe he's starting to realise that he needs someone after all?'

She shook her head, as always so dismissive of her husband's latest bright idea that he felt slighted by her mere presence. 'Pangborne doesn't strike me as the sort of bloke who spooks easily,' she said.

'You reckon?'

'Harry, he's a wide boy. You said that yourself, after he sacked you.'

'It was just a thought…'

She continued loading the dishwasher. 'I think you'd be better applying the grey matter elsewhere. How'd you feel about what I suggested last night?'

'What… re-training? At my age?'

'You're only 43.'

'I don't suppose there's anything going at your place?'

'Yes… if you're happy stacking shelves all day. But that's not going to help us pay the mortgage any more than you collecting benefits, is it? You've got to get yourself a new career. Something lucrative.'

Harry stumped up and down the kitchen. He was a big, burly man – too burly really; he'd allowed himself to go to seed in the last couple of years. His belly hung over his jeans waistband. His beard and moustache were grey and scraggy.

'You'd think there'd be some security work out there in this day and age, wouldn't you?' he complained.

'There probably is… for ex-coppers who didn't leave the job under a cloud.'

Harry frowned helplessly. There was no argument with that.

'Harry… if you want to do something useful, go and tidy the living room. It looks like a bomb's hit it.'

'I'll just go up and check my emails first. See if anyone's got back to me.'

'No one will have got back to you,' she called after him. 'It's past six.'

Harry knew that would be true even before he flopped down in front of his computer screen, wherein his inbox still read 'Empty'. It always read 'Empty' unless someone was spamming him. He hit one of his bookmarks. A colourful image unfolded onscreen. It was a collage of different pictures, each one portraying a man or woman, of varied age and ethnicity, and all in the throes of happiness as they got on with whatever job they'd been photographed doing: from laying bricks to inputting data, from serving food to driving wagons.

Emblazoned across the top was the legend:

PEOPLEFIND
Filling London's job needs
Supplying labour where you need it, when you need it

In the top right-hand corner, one picture depicted an improbably handsome guy in his early thirties. His crisp blond locks were crammed under a PVC hardhat, and he was carrying a clipboard. He was on a building site somewhere, and was gazing upward, laughing, showing a row of perfect, pearly white teeth.

'One of these days, Pangborne,' Harry said under his breath. 'Who knows? Maybe even *today*.'

Chapter
2

'Now that's impressive,' Rory said.

The space platform was about fifteen miles in diameter. It was an immense floating citadel covered by a translucent shield-dome. Its myriad buildings were towering crystalline structures, each one tapering to a needle point. They'd have looked like natural formations had it not been for the arrays of glittering, multicoloured lights running through their interiors: neon blue, Day-Glo orange, aqua-green. On the platform's surface, narrow passages wound between the high-rise edifices; these too were a mass of colours and glaring light, tiny matchstick figures thronging along them. Gigantic, glyph-like lettering was everywhere, pulsating with colour: on hoardings and overarching walkways, on the sides of buildings, on egg-shaped, aerial craft – dirigibles possibly – moving lazily back and forth through the dome's high spaces.

'And that's only one of them,' the Doctor said, joining

Amy and Rory in front of the TARDIS monitor screen. 'There are fifty like that on the Outer Rim.'

'And what did you call it?' Amy said, fascinated. 'A "leisure platform"?'

'That's right. There are forty on the Inner Rim as well. But out here is where it really gets wild and woolly.'

She glanced at him. 'They throw a good party?'

'They throw nothing but parties.' The Doctor pursed his lips. 'Of course, when you say "good", it all depends whether you mean "good" as in morally acceptable, or as in unrelenting, intense and everyone getting their money's worth.'

Amy shrugged, as if either would work for her.

'Ninety non-stop parties,' Rory said. 'Sounds like overkill to me.'

The Doctor shrugged. 'Oh, I don't know. Work hard, play hard. That's the Torodon motto. We're all owed our chill-out time. Chilling out is... cool.'

'So, are we going there?' Amy asked, trying to sound as if she wasn't excited by the prospect.

'Yes,' the Doctor said. 'But there's a slight proviso. A condition-ette.'

'Isn't there always?' she grumbled.

'The Torodon are not very modern in their outlook. The men do all the industrial work, and nearly all the Torodon females you'll find down there...' and he raised and wiggled his eyebrows meaningfully, 'will be working in the entertainment business.'

'Ahhh...'

'In various capacities. Dancing, waitressing, bartending... But it's a man's world, if you know what I mean. So you,' and he looked at Amy, 'will need to watch your step.'

'Don't worry about me,' she retorted. 'If some bloke thinks he's going to treat me like…'

'Pond!' The Doctor pointed a stern but warning finger. 'Let's not go there. We take alien races as we find them. Well, unless they're invading some poor defenceless planet. Or developing dangerous time-travel technology. Or…' He waved his hand as if to dismiss the distraction. 'Anyway, the point is that eventually they'll see the error of their ways, but it's not our responsibility to make that change for them.'

The Doctor turned to Rory. 'For the same reason, these Outer Rim platforms also attract people who are not involved in honest work. I'm talking smugglers, gamblers – all kinds of criminals. So *you'll* need to watch your step as well.'

Rory sniffed. 'Perhaps this isn't such a good idea?'

The Doctor moved to the console. 'You can stay in the TARDIS if you want. But this particular platform, LP9, is policed by an old friend of mine. He won't let things get too out of hand. If we mind our manners and keep a low profile, everything should be fine. In fact, it should be quite an experience. Think of it as being like a galactic Wild West town.'

'Who is your old friend?' Amy wondered. 'Wyatt Earp?'

The Doctor smiled. 'He makes Wyatt Earp look like a nursery teacher.'

'Typical,' she said. 'There's always someone who has to spoil things.'

Chapter

3

That night, Harry took pains to disguise himself, using boot polish to darken his beard and moustache, and pulling on a woolly black cap, black knitted gloves and a heavy donkey jacket.

He made these preparations in front of the living room mirror, because Dora wasn't there. As was her way midweek, she'd dozed for most of the evening on the settee, before heading up to bed at around nine o'clock.

Sophie wasn't around either. Earlier that evening, she'd grudgingly replied to her mother's phone calls to say that she was 'going with Baz to a gig'. When asked by Dora how she was paying for it (and presumably for Baz), Sophie had replied that she'd be using her EMA, despite its main purpose being to aid with her travel costs to and from college. This was something she didn't want to do but had no choice about, she said, her tone implying that it was all her parents' fault for not giving her an extra allowance. When Dora had replied that Sophie ought to get a part-time job like most of her friends, Sophie had cut the call.

Harry wasn't concerned. He'd long ago given up trying to impose discipline on his daughter; her scornful defiance of everything he said had reminded him once too often of his own inadequacies. Likewise, he'd stopped being exasperated by the calm manner with which his wife accepted Sophie's wayward lifestyle. If Dora wanted to believe that this unprovoked rebelliousness was genuinely nothing more than 'an assertion of teen independence', that was up to her. For the moment, he was simply glad the two them weren't around to interfere.

He picked up his holdall. It contained a rope and grapple, an electric torch, a pair of bolt-cutters, a screwdriver, a roll of duct tape and some surgical gloves: in short, a burglary kit. His spine chilled as the reality of what he was doing washed over him.

He'd been a police officer for eighteen years; he'd given law enforcement the best part of his life. It was difficult to see how he had finally come to *this*.

Two voices argued inside his head. One said that he was taking too much of a risk. Regardless of the rights and wrongs, getting caught tonight would be the last thing he'd need; it would give him a criminal record at a time when he was trying to get back on his feet. The other contested that risks were sometimes necessary. He'd taken countless as a cop; he'd bent the rules on numerous occasions during his service, and it had helped him secure some of his best arrests. And this would be no different. OK, he'd be forcing entry to someone else's property, and doing damage; by the letter of the law, yes, he *would* be committing burglary. But this was an end to a greater means. If he could show Grant Pangborne that he needed a security man on the site – a week before ringing up and asking for his old job back – it had to be worth it.

The longest unbroken stretch of the journey there was on the Circle Line. At this late hour, Harry rode in his compartment alone. One deserted platform after another flickered by, scrap paper blowing in the breeze. He only saw handfuls of commuters: the odd gang of teenagers; the occasional dishevelled businessman. Not the sort he'd expect a problem from, but even so he couldn't help wondering if they suspected that he was up to no good. Maybe all villains felt this way when going to do a job.

A job.

Again, he went cold.

He reminded himself what had happened with Peoplefind. He'd been out of the police a year when he'd put in his application form to them. They were a private recruitment agency, who specialised in allocating unskilled and semi-skilled labour across the capital. Most of the time they were only able to provide applicants with short or part-time contracts, but this was better than earning nothing. Even so, Harry, with his track record, hadn't expected that they'd be able to help him. But after only one interview with Grant Pangborne – the MD of Peoplefind – he'd been startled to be offered work on the site itself, providing security. It was a surprise they hadn't already hired someone to fill that role. Presumably they previously hadn't thought there'd be anything on site to make it worth a thief's while breaking in, though most likely insurance issues had finally necessitated that they appoint someone.

Harry had still worried that Pangborne would be

deterred from employing him by the circumstances of his enforced departure from the Met, but far from it. Apparently, Pangborne had felt that Harry was 'just the right man' – what exactly that meant when Harry had such a tainted record was difficult to fathom. But of course he'd taken the job, and everything had gone swimmingly for the next three months. He'd worked to the best of his ability, scrutinising everyone who came on site, keeping accurate records, even attempting to arrange the installation of CCTV and a better alarm system.

Maybe it was his imagination, but it was this last thing that had seemed to tip the balance against him. During the course of the three months, the more efficient Harry had been the more frustrated he felt Grant Pangborne had become with his performance. When his initial contract had expired, Pangborne had shown no hesitation in informing Harry that they wouldn't be renewing it. They'd decided that having a full-time security officer at such a small depot was an expensive luxury.

Even now, Harry was bewildered. Grant Pangborne, who wore a Rolex watch and only the most chic Armani suits, and who arrived at his office each morning in a Bentley, had never struck him as being financially strapped. Of course, rich men didn't get rich by spending money unless they absolutely needed to. Well – and about this Harry suddenly felt grimly determined – Grant Pangborne was about to wake up to the reality of *need*.

Chapter
4

The Torodon were basically humanoid, with two legs, two arms, a head, torso and so on. But they were of larger, stockier build than the average human, and moved with leonine grace – even the women's physiques suggested impressive strength. They had shaggy white hair and a silvery skin-tone, both of which contrasted sharply with their piercing blue eyes.

Most Torodon males wore a basic bodysuit of shiny, elastic material, but over the top of that all kinds of extra, heavy-duty clothing: capes and bandoliers, hauberks that were belted and harnessed, clumping, steel-clad boots and thick woollen leggings. From the scuffs and stains that streaked these rough-and-ready garments, they were work uniforms. Evidently, those wearing them were here taking a break from whatever mine, factory or space refinery they toiled in. The Torodon females wore considerably less, in many cases little more than the figure-hugging bodysuits, but also stiletto heels and rainbow-coloured facial make-up that would not have been out of place on Earth during the 1980s. They dripped with jewellery, and wore their hair dyed and styled with astonishing extravagance.

That said, three plainly dressed strangers didn't attract much attention.

'No one's batted an eyelid at us,' Rory said, as they threaded along a noisy street.

The Doctor shrugged. 'The Torodon Confederation spans several star systems, and they exploit all their natural resources. That means they have a colossal workload, and not enough workers. So they import loads of immigrant labour.'

It was true that there were different species loitering around: reptilians, insectoids. There was also a very diminutive group – hunched, shrewish figures, grey-skinned and often with distorted features – who limped about, pushing carts or carrying packages. One blundered into them, and Amy grimaced when she saw him up close; his facial features were badly malformed – they'd almost melted into each other.

'Ex-convict,' the Doctor said, once the pathetic figure had hurried on his way. 'The Torodon have always used convict labour. Any planet where they have implemented heavy industry, there are work camps. These are the remnants of those who worked the sulphur quarries on Gorgoror. The neuro-toxins in the air eventually had a catastrophic effect.'

'Those creatures were once Torodon?' Amy asked, horrified.

'It's no surprise there were riots,' the Doctor said. 'The Gorgoror prison facility was destroyed more than once by its inmates. The final uprising was interrupted by a major earthquake, so the whole complex had to close permanently. But there were plenty of emergencies before that. The last convicts were sent to these Outer Rim leisure platforms to work as menials. They still don't have much of a life.'

'I'm not sure I like the Torodon,' Amy said.

'Oh, every race has skeletons in its closets. In the case of the Bone Hoarders of Nebulo Beta, quite literally in fact. But don't be too quick to judge.'

Every few metres, arched entrances gave through to spacious interiors filled with lurid lighting and wild shouting. No doubt these were bars, nightclubs, casinos and so on. Outside them, flamboyantly clad Torodon girls catcalled to the men. There were similarly tacky displays on the street: rickety stalls gaudily coloured and crammed with curios, displays of impromptu street theatre, in which jugglers performed alongside acrobats and fire-eaters. Every so often, Torodon police officers would press through the crowd in globular, visored helms and body armour consisting mainly of articulated black plate.

Like everyone else, the cops seemed oblivious to the rainwater streaming off them. Both Rory and Amy, on stepping outside the TARDIS, had been stunned to find themselves in an intense downpour, which was clearly a regular occurrence given the numerous gutters cut into the platform's floorways.

'Not rain,' the Doctor had explained. 'Condensation. From the underside of the dome roof. Like I said, this is the Outer Rim of the Phrygian system. LP9 only services workers from the most far-flung planets and asteroids. It's *cold* out there.'

They entered what looked like a central plaza. It was as crowded as everywhere else, but its far end was dominated by an official-looking building. All its windows were of opaque glass, and a sweeping flight of steps, built from shining marble, let to its entrance, which was located under a portico pillared with stone.

'Government House,' the Doctor said. 'So ostentatious only a mayor could be found here. Not to mention a law court. And also, of course, Police Headquarters.'

'And why are we going to the police, again?' Rory asked.

'Kobal Zalu and I go back some time,' the Doctor recalled. 'He was a soldier once. We served together.'

Amy looked round at him. '*You* were a soldier?'

'More a consultant than a squaddie.' The Doctor was thoughtful. 'Torodon was at war at with the Terileptils. There was a particularly nasty space battle, and the TARDIS got caught in the crossfire. I finished up on a damaged Torodon destroyer, where I had to fix lots of fiddly stuff before we all got blown to bits. Never managed to repair the coffee machine, mind you – which some of them weren't too impressed by. Anyway, Zalu was on board. He was young then – a lieutenant in the Galactic Marine Corps. His group were off on a mission on the comet Zamos. If I hadn't helped out, they wouldn't have managed it.' He walked towards the official building. 'Since we happened to be in this part of space-time, it seemed like a chance to call in for a cuppa with an old mucker. But...' He halted again. 'There's nothing more boring than reminiscing about old times when they're old times you didn't share in, is there? Why don't you two just flutter off? See the sights? There's plenty to do here.'

Amy grabbed Rory's arm. 'Sounds like a plan.'

'Just try to avoid trouble,' the Doctor reminded them.

'That sounds like a plan too,' Rory said. He firmly linked arms with Amy before they sauntered away.

The Doctor turned back towards Government House. He'd learned from bitter experience that hooking up with old pals wasn't always the best policy. But he'd seen Kobal Zalu many times since the war with the Terileptils, and, as far as he was aware, he'd left him a contented and grateful man. Things had been good between them.

At which point he was hailed by a siren-like voice from above.

Hovering overhead was a long, sleek aircraft, black in colour and bulbous at one end. It was covered with police insignia.

'I said don't move!' the voice bellowed.

With a pneumatic hiss, a hatch slid open in the craft's underside and, before the Doctor could object, he felt a terrific suction and went rocketing upward. The next thing, he was tucked inside a narrow, padded capsule. Another hatch slid open. The featureless visor of a police officer gazed in at him.

'Hello,' the Doctor said. 'Um, could you tell me what I'm being arrested for?'

The policeman ignored him. Instead, he addressed someone else – most likely a partner seated at the flight controls. 'This is him. I'm certain of it.'

'I'm pretty sure I have a right to know,' the Doctor protested.

'Keep quiet!' the cop snapped. 'You're lucky you haven't been shot on sight.'

Chapter
5

Harry had never expected that it would be so easy to get into Peoplefind.

He'd walked up to the front door and, even dressed as he was, no one had looked twice as he'd tapped in the key-code and entered. Once inside, all he'd had to do was deactivate the alarm, and that was it. On first setting out from home he'd expected that he'd have to climb over the rear wall, or something, hence the rope and grapple. He'd been working on the basis that the entry codes would both have been changed by now, and it astonished him that neither had been.

The red eyes of the alarm censors watched him harmlessly as he moved from room to room, but without CCTV backup what use were they? His basic plan, once inside, had been to start smashing computer terminals, though he didn't like the idea of doing that. Besides, he'd have to think things through a little more carefully now. If it was apparent to the investigating officers who came in the morning that the offender had come in through the front door, they'd know it was an inside job. And it wouldn't take them long to focus on a former security guard disgruntled because he'd been sacked. So, before he did anything else, he'd have to set up a fake point of entry, probably somewhere at the rear, to make this look like the work of an opportunistic vandal.

The yard at the rear was about fifty metres by forty, the encircling wall almost four metres high. That would take some climbing, even with a rope and grapple – however, there was also a double-gate by which vehicles were allowed access. This was only two and a half metres high and, though there were barbed-wire coils along its top, Harry could pull some down and make it look as if he'd gained entry that way. He slid out through the offices' rear door. There was a motion-sensitive arc-light high in the southeast corner. He had a vague idea where its field of vision started and ended. If he first edged his way along the south wall and after that along the west, he should reach the gate without activating it.

But then he received a shock. During the time he'd spent here, he'd never known a vehicle be parked in the yard at night. Yet now there were two of them. By their size they were lorries, though it was difficult to tell as they were covered by tarpaulins.

Harry tried to recompose himself. This wouldn't make any difference. In fact, maybe it would help. He could damage the vehicles as well, so it would really look like wanton vandalism. He was edging along the wall when he heard the first muffled cry for help. Harry froze, wondering if he'd imagined it.

When the second cry came, he realised that it was

close – whoever it was, they were on the premises with him, though again the voice had been muffled as if it was indoors. He peered across the yard at the depot garage. It was closed. The windows in its office were in darkness. He hardly dared walk out into the centre of the yard to look, because that would trigger the arc-light. But then he heard a third cry. Incredulous, Harry regarded the two shrouded vehicles.

Someone was inside one of the wagons.

A different voice now shouted. Suddenly there was a hubbub, as if the captives had realised there was somebody outside.

'No wonder you don't want a security guard, Pangborne,' Harry said as he ventured forward. 'No wonder you don't want CCTV.'

He was no longer concerned about the light. He doubted it was even operational – and he was right. He entered its field of vision, and it didn't activate. He hurried to the rear end of the nearest vehicle. Was this what Peoplefind was really about? The irony of that name! Pangborne was smuggling in illegal workers, maybe illegal migrants.

Harry dumped his bag and took out his bolt-croppers. He'd still have to play this cutely. Uncovering a racket like this would stand him in good stead, but he'd have to explain why he'd been on private property at the time. No matter. First he had to release these poor wretches. Heaven knew what conditions they'd been transported in. He lifted the tarpaulin. It was no surprise to see a registration plate originating from eastern Europe. Above this was a timber door-ramp fastened with chains.

'Hey!' he shouted. 'Can you hear me?'

There was a renewed gabble of voices.

Harry fitted the bolt-cropper blades around a link in the first chain – only for a hand to grab the back of his neck with crushing force.

Harry Mossop was a big, heavy man, but now was lifted bodily into the air.

And then he was flung.

He somersaulted across the yard, landing on the tarmac with pile-driving force. He lay face down for several seconds, before looking groggily up. The tarpaulin at the back of the second vehicle had also been lifted, revealing another door-ramp – though this was lowered and of very different design from the first. It was made of smooth steel and oval in shape. The entrance behind it gave off a shimmering blue glow.

A massive silhouette stepped in front of it.

Harry tried to wriggle away as the figure came forward with echoing footfalls. It was a man wearing heavy-duty clothing – some kind of shiny body-armour, but he was at least two metres tall.

Once again Harry was grabbed and swung up into the air. His protests became meaningless blather on sight of the face that regarded him.

Firstly, it was so oddly angled that it seemed to have been stretched over an artificial skull. Secondly, it was in two sections, neither of which looked as if they'd been their owner's original property. The left side of the face was that of a younger man who'd suffered illness and injury; its skin silver-grey in colour, but wrinkled and pockmarked. The right side might once have belonged to a woman; it was smoother in tone, its features more refined, yet it was pallid, in fact dead-white, as if it had never quite adhered to the tissue below. The two halves

were joined in the centre by a line of lumpy scar-tissue –
the remnant of crude sutures – which ran up across the
chin, through the mouth, bisected the nose and passed
between the eyes, before continuing across the top of the
hairless cranium, where tiny gaps showed glints of metal
beneath.

Two eyes bored into Harry from different shaped
sockets; they were like steel points, swivelling in unison
as if attached to a machine.

'Do you like my face?' a bass, bell-like voice asked.

Harry could only stutter.

'When it was blown off, they didn't have a complete
spare they could replace it with, so they had to cannibalise
dismembered corpses. I could have had it replaced at a
later date, more professionally. But I don't know… I think
battlefield repairs have a kind of romance about them.'
The two-faced horror snickered. 'And they're more than
you'll be getting.'

Harry was flung through the air again, but this time
ripped at his assailant's sleeve as he went, stripping it
loose – revealing a limb composed of what looked like
rods and springs. Harry never really had time to absorb
this. He hit the perimeter wall with sledgehammer
force, the blow to the back of his head jolting him out of
consciousness. The last thing he remembered was a pair
of giant boots stumping forward with enough weight and
power to pulverise his flesh.

Chapter
6

Rory and Amy were in the midst of an alien culture, but they were also in a gaming hall, and the emphasis here seemed the same as in gaming halls on Earth – in that everything was glitzy and tasteless. The predominant colours on the tiled floors, wall-hangings and tubular handrails were gold and silver. Earthenware pots were located at regular intervals, and from each one a towering mass of exotic but painfully imitation foliage reached up to astonishing height. Waitresses pirouetted everywhere on preposterously high heels, wielding trays overloaded with drinks. The noise was deafening, consisting of weird and, to human ears at least, tuneless music, but it was also filled with a clangour of bells, whistles and braying laughter.

Some games were instantly recognisable. A giant screen hung above a platform, and on it there were sporting events. Rory was fascinated by what appeared to be a steeplechase over a sandy plain, in which ape-like jockeys rode the backs of lumbering sauropods. On the platform, an obese, bare-chested Torodon was giving the odds in classic bookie fashion. An excitable horde had gathered, waving wads of paper money. There were also Torodon versions of slot machines; players seated in front of screens on which images spun in kaleidoscopic fashion. Every so often they would shout a command, and the images would freeze. Some players would disappointedly lurch away, but others would laugh and shout as they hit a switch and received a plastic tab, which registered their winnings.

Once again, there were advertisements everywhere: electronic banners running back and forth across screens hanging from the ceilings, or even appearing as holographs, three-dimensional figures popping up in the middle of the floor, offering products or talking about the latest shows to hit town. One face Amy saw again and again belonged to a Torodon called Zubedai. She suspected he was a kind of pop star, as he was the only male she'd seen wearing facial make-up, and his white hair was styled; it frizzed out into a wild, 1970s-style afro. A few seconds later, she saw him for real. He was wrapped in a heavy fleece and hurrying across the gaming hall, a Torodon female on each arm. Though a celebrity, he wasn't drawing too much interest from the punters, which seemed to be the way of it on LP9, where informality was the rule. Interspersed with the raucous crowds, both Rory and Amy had spotted numerous Torodon who, by their dress and manner, were better heeled than the riff-raff surrounding them. As the Doctor had said, there was a big market for entertainment here. No doubt these were performers, managers, agents – and yet they moved freely without being harassed (unless you counted the attention of beautiful Torodon women as harassment, which Rory didn't think he did).

'Once you've seen one casino, you've seen 'em all,' Amy said. 'Are we going?'

Rory nodded, but as they headed towards the nearest exit, he noticed an oval marble table with a raised rim. A black cloth was laid over its surface, written with odd lettering and marked with a series of connected gold boxes. Another bunch of excited Torodon were standing around it, throwing what looked like dice. At one end of the table, a non-Torodon – a bipedal reptilian, with fawn-coloured skin covered in large brown blotches – but dressed in a bright blue uniform with gold braid, was acting as dealer.

'Looks like Craps,' Rory said.

'And?' Amy replied.

She'd been the keenest among them to come down here, but was already bored. She was half-wondering if there might be a show they could catch. She mentioned this, but Rory ambled over to the table.

'Told you,' he said. 'I mean superficially it's different, but it's the same type of game. There's the Pass Line, there's the Don't Pass Bar.'

The dice were not dissimilar to Earth dice in that they were small cubes, though they bore glyph-like figures rather than patterns of dots. The dealer watched calmly, his green tongue occasionally flickering. One particular player – a sleek, handsome Torodon, wearing a billowing silk gown similar to a kimono, and his long, white hair tied in a topknot almost like a samurai – rolled again and again. Other players placed their betting chips on different sections of the table; some were winning, others losing, but the 'shooter' – as Rory thought of him – was clearing up every time. Several other Torodon were with him; big, brutal characters in mismatched garb that looked more like space armour than work clothing. One by one the other players drifted away, but the successful shooter was hardly concerned. He'd now amassed a mountain of chips.

'That bloke's almost too good to be true,' Rory said quietly, though it wasn't quietly enough. The shooter glanced across the table, suddenly noticing there were humans present.

'You implying something?' he asked, though he sounded relaxed rather than angry.

'You keep on winning,' Rory pointed out.

'Really… I must've missed that.'

There were chuckles from around the table.

'What I mean is… this is a game of chance,' Rory said. 'We have something like it on Earth. It takes a bit of skill, but it's mainly about luck. Which makes it strange that you keep winning.'

Amy tugged at his arm. 'Why don't we just go?'

'You accusing me of cheating?' the shooter said. He still didn't sound angry, but he now leaned forward, and Amy saw hard lines of muscle beneath his gown.

'It doesn't matter,' Rory said, backing away, but when he and Amy turned to leave, others of the shooter's compatriots had circled behind them.

'How exactly could I cheat?' the shooter asked.

'I didn't say you cheated,' Rory replied.

'It's clear what you meant. So I ask again… how could I cheat?'

Rory shrugged. 'On Earth, they sometimes use weighted dice.'

The shooter rolled the dice across the table. 'Do these feel weighted to you?'

Rory didn't bother to pick them up. 'I wouldn't know. I'm not an expert.'

'But you talk as if you are.' The shooter now gazed at Rory with eerie intensity.

'Look, pack it in with the tough-guy gambler act, eh!' Amy snapped. 'Can't you see, we're not interested?'

The shooter smiled again. 'This one lets his woman fight his battles for him?'

There was ribald laughter. Rory felt his cheeks flush.

'Come on.' Amy grabbed Rory's arm and led him from the table, shouldering her way through the heavies half-blocking their path.

'You *had* better walk away, friend,' the shooter said after them. 'You're way past any help we can give you.'

Again, there was laughter. Rory's brow burned, and before he knew it he'd spun back around. He wasn't the inexperienced wimp he'd once been, he reminded himself. He'd seen things that even space rodents like these couldn't dream of.

The shooter feigned surprise. 'Whoa… so you've got some fight in you, after all. Enough to take me on?'

Rory licked his lips. He was still aware of Amy tugging at him.

'No need to look scared,' the shooter said. 'I mean across the table. And if you doubt my dice…' he indicated a bowl where some spare dice were kept, 'we can use different ones.'

Rory was tempted. He was *so* tempted. But he didn't

know the rules of this game. 'I've nothing to bet with,' he finally said. 'We're not carrying Torodon money.'

'He doesn't fight his own battles or carry his own money,' the shooter proclaimed. 'We must be in the presence of royalty.'

There was more laughter.

'We're just visiting,' Rory said through clenched teeth.

'You don't have to explain yourself to these people,' Amy hissed.

'I think he does,' the shooter said. 'Look at him… He yearns to accept my challenge. He's itching for it. Xurgan, loan him some credits.'

One of the shooter's lackeys pushed a handful of plastic chips across the table.

'On which we'll owe you 600 per cent interest, no doubt,' Rory said.

The shooter regarded him carefully, maybe realising that this Earthman wasn't such a dullard after all. 'In that case… this isn't a loan, it's a gift. You hear that everyone? This is a gift.' He smiled at Rory again. 'Now you've got no excuse.'

Rory groped the chips towards him.

'Don't be stupid,' Amy said. 'You can't play this game.' She indicated the alien symbols. 'You don't even know what these figures represent.'

'I have a translation device, sir,' the reptilian dealer said. He produced what looked like a pair of sunglasses, though they were rimmed with complex instrumentation. His fingers had soft pads on their tips, but he ran them nimbly across a row of lights on the device's left arm, and handed it over.

Tentatively, Rory put the glasses on. Everything he now saw was slightly shaded – but when he focused on the table he was looking at recognisable Earth numerals. On the dice, the glyphs had given way to straightforward numbers, one through to six.

'This is great,' he said.

'For heaven's sake,' Amy retorted.

'Well?' the shooter asked. 'Do we play?'

Rory glanced at his wife. 'How hard can it be?'

'On *your* head, Rory Williams. And those goggles are ridiculous. You look like Elton John.'

'You've got yourself a game,' Rory said to his opponent.

'Excellent,' the shooter replied. 'Dead Man's Duel… You understand?'

'No, of course we don't!' Amy snapped, not liking the sound of that at all.

The shooter stared at Rory. 'Only two of us can play. No one else may bet.'

Rory nodded. 'That's fine.'

Amy wondered if it was her imagination that their audience was suddenly holding its breath. Surely that wouldn't be their normal response to a measly game of Craps? Even one of the grey-skinned menials – a shrivelled figure wearing a work-belt hung with tools, was leaning on a broom to watch.

The shooter rubbed his hands together. 'Good. Let's play.'

39

Chapter
7

'Who are you?' the two-faced giant roared. His voice was deep and, again, bell-like – as if issuing from a pair of iron lungs.

Harry was fastened onto an upright rack, his wrists and ankles held in vice-like rings. He was inside the second vehicle, though plainly it was no HGV. Powerful blue lights glared from all sides, preventing him seeing clearly. His captor wasn't alone – he had a sidekick – a short, stocky version of himself, without the facial scars and with a mane of white hair cut square at his shoulders.

'I've already told you,' Harry wept. 'Harry Mossop. I used to work here as a security guard.'

'Why are you here *now*?' the terrible voice demanded.

'I… suspected Pangborne was up to something,' Harry stammered.

This was a lie of course, but Harry felt he had to tell them something they'd believe; in the face of this aggression, his real reasons seemed too pathetic to be true.

'*Why* did you suspect?' his interrogator bellowed.

'I couldn't think of any reason why Pangborne would have got rid of me and not replaced me.'

'How did you know he hadn't replaced you?'

'Look… please, what is this?'

'*Answer the question!*'

'I've been observing his operation.'

There was a brief silence as his captors exchanged glances.

'Observing?' the shorter one queried. 'How long for?'

'What does it matter?'

The giant leaned down until his mutilated nose was less than an inch from Harry's. 'It matters because we need to know if you've passed information to anyone else!'

'I haven't.'

'I'd like to believe you, Earthman… I really would.'

'I promise you I haven't!'

'*Tell us the truth!*' the shorter one shouted, producing a loose wire, the end of which was glowing hot.

'I am telling the truth!' Harry wailed.

The short one gestured with the wire, and, for a hellish second, Harry imagined it was about to be plunged into his right eye. But this never happened. The would-be torturer contemplated this act, but at length turned to his giant companion. 'We've no time for this, Zarbotan. Any security breach is a breach too many.'

'I agree.'

'So we leave straightaway, yes?'

'No.' The giant tapped out digits on a hanging screen.

'Zarbotan!' the other objected.

'Don't be a fool!' Zarbotan replied. 'Krauzzen would want us to be thorough.'

On the screen, swirling static coalesced into an image. Harry blinked at the sight of Grant Pangborne – now, for some reason, wearing silver face make-up. He was dressed in a fluffy gown and reclining on a couch, probably in his penthouse in Docklands.

'What is it?' Pangborne asked tiredly.

'Xorax!' Zarbotan said. 'What do you know of this fellow?'

Pangborne sat up. Harry realised that he was looking back through the screen at them. 'That's Mossop. I had him at my depot as a security officer.'

'We now have him at your depot as an intruder,' Zarbotan said.

'An intruder?'

'It seems you've been getting sloppy, Xorax. We caught him snooping.'

'I should have known better than to employ an ex-policeman.'

'A policeman!' the smaller captor exclaimed.

Pangborne tried to play this down. 'It's nothing to worry about, Zalizta. Mossop was the worst kind of policeman. Lazy, incompetent. I inquired into his background, and when they terminated his employment they were glad to see the back of him.'

'Nevertheless,' Zarbotan said, 'if he's spoken to other policemen…?'

'He won't have. He has no contact with them any more.'

'He claims to have been investigating you,' Zalizta said.

Pangborne laughed. 'I sincerely doubt that. Knowing Mossop, this will have been some ham-fisted attempt to get his old job back. I wouldn't worry.'

'It's *you* who should be worried, Xorax,' Zarbotan replied.

Harry struggled to comprehend what he was hearing; none of it boded well.

'Now, wait.' Pangborne said, looking alarmed. 'I've kept my end of the bargain. There were always going to be risks on a planet like Earth. I've told you before. It isn't easy to make humans disappear without questions being asked.'

'Save it for Lord Krauzzen,' Zarbotan said.

'This is absurd!' Pangborne protested.

'No more absurd than it would be if we ignored this security breach.'

'Zarbotan!' Pangborne shouted. 'Xorg needs me.'

'Like he needs a crack in the hull of the *Ellipsis*!'

'Let me prove it. That fellow there, Mossop. You can't just take him. He has a family who'll miss him.'

Zarbotan glanced at Harry, who felt a new depth of chill.

'See for yourself,' Pangborne said, lifting a keyboard to his knee.

Rows of digits flowed across the screen. Zarbotan and Zalizta perused them.

'Zarbotan, please!' Harry begged. 'Not my family!'

'I've never been inclined to separate loved ones,' Zarbotan said at length. 'Put him with the rest of the product.

'You leave my family alone, do you hear!'

'I hear,' Zarbotan said dismissively. A hatch-like

door slid open in front of him, revealing an antechamber packed with incomprehensible, neon-lit gadgetry.

As Zalizta did something to the rear of the rack, and his manacles sprang loose, Harry leapt to his feet. 'I'll show you how incompetent I am!'

He aimed a punch at Zalizta, who was struck on the shoulder and knocked backwards. Harry swung around, looking for an exit, only for Zarbotan's mechanical hand to clamp round his throat. Harry choked and gargled as again he was lifted from his feet. Zarbotan glared up at him, odd-shaped eyes gleaming with unnatural light.

'Earthman… if you have no concern for yourself, think about your family. You have already condemned them. But every action you take from here on will dictate how much, or how little, they suffer.'

Chapter
8

Things went well for Rory at first.

It was, as he'd surmised, similar to the Earth game of Craps. All he had to do was wager on the outcome of the roll of a dice. He shot carefully, sticking to the etiquette he remembered from the movies: shaking in one hand, rolling cleanly down the table, ensuring the dice hit the back wall. It seemed to pay off. He won the first four rounds, choosing to bet *with* the dice, and each time doubling his money. His opponent was unconcerned by this. He was even complimentary.

'You're a natural,' he said.

Rory was acutely aware of Amy's disapproving presence, though she was watching with increased interest. More Torodon had gathered around the table, and were equally engrossed. Having amassed quite a pile of chips, Rory opted to press his bets, rolling past the point and doubling his money again.

And then, suddenly, his luck seemed to change.

He threw under the point and, for the first time, lost.

'That's unfortunate,' his opponent said, reclaiming all the bets for himself and taking charge of the dice.

Slowly but steadily, Rory watched his pile of chips dwindle, until, perhaps inevitably, he was placing his final bet. The gathered crowd were still rapt. He found this confusing. It was hardly a big deal; this had never been his money to lose in the first place.

'Reparation throw?' his opponent asked.

'What's a "reparation throw"?' Amy asked suspiciously. She glanced towards the menial with the broom; he might only have been a janitor, but he clearly understood the way things worked here, because he was shaking his head.

'Just do it,' Rory said tensely, having placed his final bet. Surely this guy couldn't win again – he'd just won nine times on the trot.

His opponent *did* win. He was throwing for an eight and that was how it came up – with two fours. Rory had heard stories that some high rollers were so skilled they could increase their chances of rolling certain numbers by the manner with which they threw. This was one reason, supposedly, why certain casinos would not allow players to bet only on their own throws. He'd thought it nonsense, but now he wasn't sure.

'This is my day, after all,' his opponent said, sweeping the table clean.

'Well played,' Rory said. He turned to Amy, nodding that it was time to leave.

'Wait!' his opponent said. 'You owe me a reparation throw.'

Rory glanced back. 'What?'

'We're playing Dead Man's Duel.'

'I don't understand.'

'The rules of the table, sir,' the dealer explained in his sibilant tone. 'In Dead Man's Duel, the loser, regardless of his financial position, must give his opponent the opportunity to claim a reparation. You *must* bet again.'

Rory showed empty hands. 'I haven't anything to stake.'

The dealer regarded him blankly. The watching crowd were silent, including the heavies gathered at Rory and Amy's back. All of a sudden the interest in this particular game was explained.

'How can we bet with something we don't have?' Amy protested.

'The normal form would be to produce an IOU,' the dealer explained. 'But it's the winner's call.'

'And I don't accept,' his opponent said. 'You're not natives of the Outer Rim. You could be anywhere in the galaxy in a month.'

'OK,' Rory said. He threw a grubby string on the table. 'I'll stake the spare bootlace I carry in my back pocket.'

His opponent laughed. 'Nice try, but not good enough. A reparation must be something of significant value. That is also in the rules. But allow me to assist. How did you come here? You must have a spacecraft.'

'Of course we have a spacecraft.'

'Rory!' Amy warned him.

Rory rounded on her. 'It's time we put this guy on his backside!'

'That's the stuff,' his opponent said. 'But you've no choice anyway. If you fail to make this bet, I can take you into servitude.'

'That'll be the day,' Rory snarled.

His opponent laughed again. One of his henchmen lumbered up with a portable monitor, on which there was an image of the LP9 landing-pads. The TARDIS occupied the foreground.

'According to the Port-Master, this is the only non-Torodon vessel in dock, Xaaael,' the henchman said. 'This must be it.'

Rory's opponent, Xaaael, glanced across the table. 'Well?'

'That's it,' Rory confirmed.

'Doesn't look like much,' the henchman said.

'She's fifty times the ship you came here in,' Rory replied.

Xaaael shrugged. 'I'll take your word for it.' He pushed his entire pile of chips forward. 'I stake everything I have against your strange-looking spacecraft.'

Rory went rigid, uncertain what to do.

'Rory, don't you dare!' Amy shouted.

Xaaael sneered at what he perceived to be Rory's henpecked status. There was something smooth and dangerous about him, but there was also something boyish and immature – as if his entire life was about winning petty victories like this.

'You're on!' Rory said.

Xaaael smiled, and shook his dice. 'Winner's privilege. This is a reparation bet, so I'm shooting on the point, and I can name my own… seven.'

Rory's heart sank. Lucky seven – though it wasn't really luck, it was just that seven had more combination possibilities from a two-dice throw than any other number between one and twelve. 'Eight,' he replied, thinking that eight and six were the next most common numbers thrown.

But the dice landed on five and two.

Xaaael laughed aloud. Rory felt faint. His 'Elton John' glasses had already ridden down his sweat-slicked nose. Now they dropped off altogether. He could still hear Amy shouting abuse in his ear, saying something about going and getting the Doctor. He stared helplessly at the two dice, willing one of them to flip over.

Xaaael came around the table, his henchmen in tow. 'Perhaps you'd like to deliver my property to me in person?'

Still dazed, Rory found himself being manhandled out of the casino in the vague direction of the LP9 landing-pads.

Chapter
9

The Doctor was alone in a pitch-black room. His sonic screwdriver had been removed, so he couldn't use it for a light. He knew that he was somewhere inside the LP9 police headquarters, but whether in a holding cell or an interrogation centre, he didn't like to speculate. He reached out with his fingers, exploring his immediate surroundings – when there was a bass, gloating chuckle.

The Doctor was dazzled as an electric blind retracted on a panoramic window, and the glitz and glamour of the leisure platform flowed in. He had to shield his eyes, so it took him a second to twig that he wasn't in a cell but in a plush office, which, as well as the usual high-tech fixtures – plasma screens streaming with data, intercom devices and so forth – was also filled with old-fashioned luxuries like leather-bound chairs and shelves lined with books.

Behind a wide desk sat a middle-aged Torodon, broad-shouldered but rather paunchy, an effect enhanced by the tight silver-blue suit he was wearing – the under-uniform normally sported by offices who weren't on outdoor duty. His head was shaven and he had a huge, walrus-like moustache, but his genial grin gave him an avuncular appearance; he could have been someone's long-lost uncle.

'Kobal Zalu,' the Doctor said. 'Well, thanks for scaring the heck out of me.'

'A Time Lord alarmed by a darkened room? Things have certainly changed. Speaking of which, I see you've changed bodies again?'

'Oh, several times since we last met.'

'Several times? Not been looking after yourself. Mind, you appear younger, which is one thing. But your dress sense hasn't improved. Sorry… preferred it when you had white hair and a pallor so ashen you could have passed for one of us.'

The Doctor pulled up a swivel chair and sat. 'My pallor was ashen because I'd just been shot out of the sky.'

'I said I was sorry for that.' Zalu smiled, though it didn't quite reach his eyes. 'Still righting wrongs wherever you go?'

'They don't tend to right themselves.' The Doctor's smile was equally wintry. 'Let me get this straight, Zalu… Your goons arrested me as a *joke*?'

Zalu rubbed his moustache with his left forefinger, a gesture familiar from his younger days – it had usually signalled that he was under pressure. 'Doctor, we need to talk. Care for a drink first?' He hit a button, and a tray slid from a wall compartment, containing a stone bottle and two crystal goblets.

'No thank you. And I'm surprised *you're* having one on duty.'

Zalu was pouring a generous measure of smoky fluid into his glass when he heard this. He whipped around. 'Don't presume to tell me my duty!' Almost immediately he became placating again. 'Not now I'm Chief of Police. It wouldn't be seemly.'

'Zalu, why do I get the impression you're not glad to see me?'

'I'm always glad to see you, Doctor. You know that.' Zalu looked sheepish. 'And for your information, this is Abadonian lemonade. But if you won't have a shot of the "hard stuff", what do you fancy?'

'I've always been partial to Torodon tea.'

'Zylva!' Zalu said into his desktop intercom. 'Tea, if you would.'

'What's the problem?' the Doctor asked.

'Problem? There's no problem.'

'You seem on edge.'

'It's been a busy day.'

The Doctor glanced around the comfortable office. 'Can't have been as busy as the average day you had when you were a colonial marshal. Those were the days, eh? Weren't they?'

'I was younger then, wilder. The Outer Rim platforms were lawless hellholes. You needed a different kind of police officer in those days.'

'Doesn't really answer my question. What's the problem?'

Zalu's strained smile faltered, as if his charade of bonhomie was becoming too much for him. 'Do you still insist on interfering everywhere you go?'

'Only where it's needed. So, OK, yes.'

'It isn't needed here.' Zalu's expression hardened.

'Look… *I'm* in charge on LP9, Doctor, and you know me well enough to understand what that means. Nothing happens here without my say-so. Whatever the rumours on the street.'

'What rumours?'

'Why have you come here?'

'To see an old friend.'

'I know you, Doctor. If you don't go looking to solve problems, you bring problems with you.'

'I've no idea what you're talking about.'

A door slid open and a Torodon female – very slim and pretty, again with rainbow-coloured hair – sashayed in, carrying a tall beaker filled with a creamily frothing brew. She placed it down.

Zalu waved her out. The door slid closed, and he rounded again on the Doctor. 'If this is genuinely a passing visit, you can drink your tea and go!'

'So nice to be made welcome.'

'Because you're *not* welcome,' Zalu asserted, though again, almost immediately, he seemed to regret it. 'I'm sorry, but what more can I say?' He produced the Doctor's sonic screwdriver and pushed it over the desktop.

The Doctor pocketed it. 'Well… I appreciate your candour.' He sipped his tea. 'And your tea. Reinvigorating as always, but there's no point in staying if I'm causing you grief.' He stood. 'And there are no biscuits. So I'll say goodbye.'

The door slid open again.

'Doctor!' Zalu said.

The Doctor turned.

'We're still friends, I hope. I'll always hold you in high regard. But I don't want you here at the present time.'

'Fair enough,' the Doctor said. 'But you didn't need to have your men rough me up and then refuse me biscuits to get that message home.'

'If they were overzealous I'll have them reprimanded.'

'I see. So… being rude to an old friend, and now punishing your underlings for carrying out your orders. Doesn't sound like the Kobal Zalu I once knew.'

'I told you, those days are over.' Zalu turned gruffly to one of his screens. 'Wherever it is you're going, safe journey.'

None the wiser, the Doctor left.

Chapter
10

When Amy left the casino, it was raining hard again, and the kaleidoscopic colours of the towering structures refracted through the downpour in an incandescent blur. Torodon folk blundered past under waterproof canopies, laughing and enjoying themselves. When she tried to speak to them, none seemed interested. Now that she needed one, there was no sign of a police officer.

'Excuse me, miss?' came a voice from behind.

She turned and saw the little, grey-skinned janitor who had watched the game. His mouth was out of shape, his eyes on different levels. The few hairs on his withered scalp were lank and lifeless. She had to resist backing away.

'Miss… you need to go with your friend.'

'Why?' she said.

'He may be in more trouble than you think.'

'He'll be in more trouble than he's ever been in in his life when I get hold of him. First, I've got to find a policeman.'

'A policeman?' The janitor looked sceptical.

'Yes. I know you have them. I've seen them.'

'There's a police help-point over there.'

He indicated a cylindrical steel tower at the junction of several thoroughfares. Amy hurried over to it. There was an arched recess at the bottom, but when she stepped inside there were no internal doors.

'Yes?' a brusque voice boomed from an intercom.

'We've just been cheated in one of the casinos.'

'You'll need to give me a little more detail.'

'My husband has got on the wrong side of some bad people. Please help us.'

With a *whooshing* rush of air, the small chamber Amy was standing in – clearly some kind of elevator – rocketed up to the top of the tower, and she found herself stepping into a small office cluttered with visual display units and complex circuitry. It looked state-of-the-art, but was stuffy and scruffy, and felt rather lived in. A Torodon police officer, clad as if for outdoor duty, spun around in a swivel chair. On seeing a non-Torodon, he removed his helmet – to reveal that he was actually a she. She had handsome but refined features. Her lustrous white hair was bound in tight coils.

'Who are you?' the officer asked.

'My name's Amy Pond, but I'm sure that… *Look!*' Amy's eyes had alighted on something over the officer's shoulder. '*There!*'

One of the screens depicted a grainy image of the landing-pads. The TARDIS sat on the nearest, and several figures were gathered around it. One of these was Rory; another was the man called Xaaael, though he'd now dispensed with his silken gown for an exoskeleton of heavy space armour. The rest of the group, his sidekicks, were equally ironclad. All now carried weapons.

'Look at their body language,' Amy said. 'You can't tell me Rory's with that lot because he wants to be.'

The officer adjusted a switch and raised the volume on that particular screen. Amy watched and listened with growing dread as one of Xaaael's larger henchmen attempted to force the TARDIS door with a crow-bar, but failed. Xaaael turned to Rory. 'Do you think us fools?'

Rory shrugged. He still looked dazed. 'I told you, I don't have a key.'

'You can't access your own spaceship?' Xaaael scoffed. 'Search him again!'

They did, slapping Rory down, turning his pockets inside out.

'Nothing,' one of them said.

Xaaael looked furious but remained calm. 'Earthman, if this is a ruse to make us leave your craft on LP9, it's backfired. All this means is that *you* come as well!'

The officer watched her screen intently.

Onscreen, Rory seemed to wake to his predicament. He tried to dart away from his captors, only for one to draw a pistol and hit him across the head.

Amy cried out as Rory slumped down unconscious.

The officer leaned forward and flicked the screen off.

'There!' Amy said. 'And you've got it all on film.'

The officer resumed on her keyboard. 'I'm sorry, there's nothing I can do.'

'What?'

'No law has been broken.'

'Are you mad?'

'If you've nothing else, you need to vacate this office. We can only deal with one complainant at a time, and someone else who needs us may be waiting below.'

'You...!' Amy said, pointing with shaking finger. 'You... I'll not forget *you*!'

Outside, she fought her way back through the crowd to the casino. To her relief, the grey-skinned janitor was still sweeping in the entrance.

'Excuse me,' she said, breathless. 'Can you tell me which way my friend went?'

The janitor glanced around, making sure no one was watching, and beckoned to her. Once inside, he led her down a side passage, at the end of which they descended a clanking steel stair into the basement area, where a conveyor belt, loaded with what looked like cargo, mostly light but sturdy aluminium crates, trundled along an arched passage of corrugated metal.

'This leads to the port,' he said. 'These supplies are bound for the *Ellipsis*.'

'*Ellipsis*?'

'The mothership to which your friend will be taken.'

'You knew they were going to abduct Rory?'

The janitor lowered his eyes. 'I've seen this happen before with visitors to LP9.'

Amy wanted to rebuke him for not speaking up at the time. But she remembered what the Doctor had said about these people being subservient, an underclass with no voice in this society.

The janitor humped one of the crates over onto the sidewalk. He took a long tool from his belt, and applied it to the lock, which sprang open. Inside the crate there were bottles containing different coloured fluids, and what looked like sealed packets of foodstuff. 'You're not a large person,' he said. 'You should be able to conceal yourself.'

Amy was incredulous. 'You want me to get inside this crate?'

'It's the only way you can help your friend.'

'I'll suffocate.'

'These cartons are not airtight. However, to make you more comfortable…'

He extricated another tool from his belt – a nail-gun of some sort – placed it against the underside of the crate and plunged the trigger. A hole was punched, about the size of a one-penny coin.

Amy backed away. 'Look, I have another friend. I'll try to find him.'

The janitor placed a hand on her harm. 'Lord Xaaael's *Raptor-Bird* will be leaving imminently. Whatever help you think you'll find on LP9 – and there's precious little – it will need to arrive very quickly.'

Amy glanced into the now half-empty crate, and then along the tunnel. This would be the craziest thing she'd ever done, but Rory was somewhere at the other end, hapless and insensible – and that should be reason enough. Ordinarily, she would go and find the Doctor, and they could follow in the TARDIS – but the TARDIS was down there as well. There was nothing else for it.

She stepped into the crate. The janitor assisted her.

'Listen,' Amy said, as she lay down and curled up. 'This other friend of mine. He's called the Doctor, and he'll come looking for me. Please tell him what's happened.'

'I will speak to him,' the janitor said, cramming packages around her.

'Hey, there's not much room in here as it is.'

'This is for ballast. So you are not injured when they throw you into the hold.'

'Great,' she said as he closed the lid. 'I'm in the ballast.'

Chapter
11

Despite her frequent annoyance with Harry, there were times when Dora Mossop fully understood the frustrations he felt about their daughter.

Such as now.

It was the early hours of the morning, and Dora had been sound asleep when her mobile had begun chirping on the bedside cabinet. She'd known it was going to be Sophie before she'd even answered the call, but perhaps it would have been less irksome if the girl had sounded distraught that Baz had dumped her for one of her friends and marooned her in Hammersmith with no money and no way to get home, rather than imparting this info in surly fashion and, instead of asking nicely if her mother could come to pick her up in the car, had emotionally blackmailed her by saying that if she couldn't get a lift she'd have no option but to walk home alone through the middle of London at this late hour.

Unable to find Harry, Dora had got dressed and driven

the ten miles to Hammersmith herself.

They were now on the way back. Sophie, who looked a mess – Dora thought she was way too old for spiked hair, Goth beads and black lace – made a sullen, unsympathetic figure, despite the eyeliner streaking her cheeks.

'So what happened?' Dora asked.

Sophie shrugged. 'Don't want to talk about it.'

Dora bit her lip. Thus far, her daughter's unwillingness to talk had also extended to an unwillingness to apologise for the inconvenience or to express gratitude.

'I've no idea where your father is,' Dora eventually said.

Sophie didn't respond to this either, as if his unexpected absence at this late hour was of no interest, which suddenly annoyed Dora no end. OK, she'd taken issue with Harry in the early days when he'd tried to put Sophie on the straight and narrow, but this was the kind of cold indifference he routinely faced from his daughter, whereas she only had to put up with it now and then because most of the time she preferred a quiet life and wouldn't voice disapproval even if she felt it.

It wasn't as if Harry had been totally unreasonable with Sophie. The main thing that bothered him about her was that, though she was now studying A levels, she wasn't showing much interest in them. Life seemed to be a non-stop party, and Sophie was enjoying it by spending money that she couldn't really afford. Perhaps he was just being a concerned father, Dora thought. But then again – where was Harry now when she needed him? It was all very well him lecturing people, but what exactly did he bring to the family these days? It was so typical that he, who had nothing to do all day, wasn't around to make this late-night journey, whereas she had to be up in the morning for work.

Frustrated, she fiddled with the heating. It was unresponsive and, in her rush to get out, Dora had neglected to put a coat on. Being late autumn, the air was frigid.

'Don't put the heating on,' Sophie said. 'I'm getting a headache, you'll just make it worse.'

'As a matter of fact,' Dora retorted. 'I—'

'*MUM!*' Sophie screamed, grabbing at the wheel.

They'd been cruising through Kensington, which at three in the morning was all but deserted, but now a glaring light filled the windscreen.

Dora grabbed the wheel back and tried to spin it. The car went into a sideways skid. It careered across the road, jolting to a halt on the opposite kerb. Intense light was still shining into the vehicle, but now from all sides.

'W-what is this?' Dora stammered.

When someone attempted to open her driver's door she clung on to it, but the strength on the other side was irresistible – in fact, the door was literally torn out of the frame of the car. A hand appeared, on the end of an arm made from articulated steel rods. As it grabbed the collar of her cardigan, Dora and her daughter shrieked.

'Zalu!' the Doctor bellowed, barging back into the Police Chief's office. 'Fancy sharing what's happening on this space platform of yours?'

Zalu looked uncomfortable as he sat behind his desk. He'd been expecting this for the last few minutes – ever since he'd read a report from one of the point-sergeants on the day-shift, and had then spotted the Doctor on a surveillance monitor, speaking animatedly with one of the service personnel.

'Doctor, I…'

'Cowering under your desks may be the new style of policing on LP9, but now my friends have gone missing, that's not going to cut it!'

Zalu's hackles rose. 'No one is cowering under their desk, Doctor.'

'Tell that to Point-Sergeant 8379 Xelos. She watched on television while my property was stolen and one of my friends got kidnapped.'

'I've already received Xelos's report. She's inquired into the incident. It seems your property was won fairly and squarely in a game of Dead Man's Duel.'

The Doctor leaned forward, and stared into Zalu's deep blue eyes. 'How can that possibly be true? I've never played Dead Man's Duel, so I can't have lost, can I? That doesn't excuse what happened next. Rory – abducted. Amy – forced to stow away on the ship where he was taken, so she's gone too.'

'You need to understand… This is a complex issue.'

'Zalu, *you* need to understand that these are my friends, and I want them back!'

'I have friends too, Doctor! And family!' Zalu stood up. 'You and your people can just disappear, but mine have to live here… do you see what I'm saying?'

The Doctor shook his head. 'Are you really the man I once knew?'

'Of course I'm not.' Zalu thumped his desk. 'How can I be? I'm not like you. I can't stay young and brave for ever.'

'You're the Chief of Police here!'

'Haven't you realised what we're dealing with, Doctor? This is organised crime. Of the most dangerous sort. You've seen where we are. Ten billion clicks outside the Inner Rim, and another twenty billion from Torodon itself. You know how it is with these Outer Rim platforms. They're infested with gangsters and racketeers. Half the casinos and nightclubs here are owned by them. Those they don't own, they skim. Their claws are sunk so deeply into local commerce that we couldn't eject them even if we had the authority to.'

'You *don't* have the authority?'

Zalu made a helpless gesture. 'They're everywhere. All around us. Involved at every level. If the various syndicates combined their powers, they'd outnumber my frontier police force a hundred to one.'

'So get reinforcements.'

'That would be expensive.'

'And the rule of crime isn't?'

'No!' Zalu seemed embarrassed by what he was now admitting. He strode around his office like a caged tiger, though a tiger minus teeth and claws. Beyond his window, the usual hordes of pleasure seekers thronged the colourful, rain-soaked streets. 'Look at this place. It's rough and ready, but, in relative terms it's pretty law-abiding.'

'I see,' the Doctor said. 'The mob polices it too. Is that what you're saying?'

'The mob – as you call them, are first and foremost businessmen. It's not in their interest for there to be serious trouble here.'

The Doctor pondered this, before smiling coldly. 'Then they made a big mistake taking one of *my* friends.'

He stormed out into the next office, only to find several younger police officers already waiting for him, pistols drawn.

'It's all right,' Zalu said, appearing behind him. 'Doctor, come with me.'

'Where to now?' the Doctor said suspiciously.

'The Intelligence Room.'

'Sounds like my sort of place.'

Zalu nodded. 'There are things you need to know.'

Chapter
12

When Dora and Sophie were dropped into the hold alongside Harry, they were numbed with shock.

It was a padded chamber, lit by a faint reddish glow. There were several people in there already, mostly foreigners, and they were just as frightened and disoriented as the Mossops. Only one of them seemed to speak English well. His name was Andrei, and he said he was from Romania.

'I'm afraid we've all been kidnapped,' he told them.

Dora and Sophie eyed Andrei uncertainly. He was tall and black-haired, and though tired and haggard, he was dark-eyed and rather handsome. He'd been wearing a fur-lined jacket, but had now taken it off because it was intensely warm. He wore a thin T-shirt beneath, which revealed a strong physique and muscular arms.

Dora turned to Harry, who'd been so relieved that his wife and daughter, though abducted, were safe, that he'd been unable to say anything and had wept as he'd cuddled them.

'Harry!' Dora said, extricating herself from his grasp. 'What's happening?'

Harry struggled to explain. 'Like this chap says… we've been kidnapped.'

'Who by?'

'I don't know.'

'But why have they taken *us*?' Sophie demanded shrilly.

'Sophie, you've got to calm down, OK?'

'Who are these people? What do they want with us?'

Harry shook his head.

Dora stared him in the eye. She could always tell when people were being evasive with her. In the early days of their marriage, her husband had often said that she'd make a better cop than him. 'Harry Mossop… what are you not telling us?'

He shrugged. 'I think it's some kind of people-trafficking operation.'

'So you *do* know what's going on?'

'I had no idea it would be like this.'

'Please don't tell me you were investigating these people.'

'No… Well, not really.'

'*Harry Mossop!* You are not a policeman any more! I appreciate you want to show your old colleagues that they made a mistake, but please don't tell me that you've got us involved with gangsters!'

Andrei butted in again. 'I think it may be worse than that.'

Dora and Sophie gazed at him, bewildered.

'How did these people abduct you?' he asked.

Dora shook her head. 'It's hard to be sure.'

'Powerful lights? Men with mechanical limbs? These are no ordinary criminals.'

'*Well this is just great!*' Sophie screamed at her father. '*You've really gone and done it this time, haven't you? You've got us all killed!*'

'Now listen,' Harry said, trying to sound firm. 'We have to stick together if we want to get through this.'

'Yeah, because sticking together has solved all our problems in the past.'

'Sophie, calm down!' Dora said.

Before more words could be exchanged, there was a thunderous vibration through the floor. It sounded like a rocket-booster had ignited beneath their feet.

The prisoners wailed and huddled together.

There was a further explosion of energy, and a tremendous g-force battered them to the floor. Their cries were lost in a storm of propulsion. Sophie sought comfort in the arms of her mother, but Dora was equally frightened. When Harry crawled towards them, Dora reluctantly let him take hold of her, but Sophie pushed him away, and, more by luck than instinct, finished up with Andrei, who wrapped her in a brawny bear-hug.

Harry knew at that moment that he'd made the worst mistake of his life. It had long been the case that almost everything he did backfired; that whenever he tried to resolve problems, he made things worse. But heaven knew what awaited them now.

'This is the offender in question,' Zalu said.

He and the Doctor were in the Intelligence Room, on a raised steel catwalk surrounded by three-dimensional screens on which visual imagery was flickering past. On the screen in front, they viewed an excerpt from police surveillance footage. It had been taken in an eatery, and it showed a lean, handsome Torodon, wearing his white hair in a topknot, seated among other diners whose faces had been blurred out.

'His name's Zagardoz Xaaael,' Zalu said. 'He's a senior lieutenant in the Xorg Krauzzen cartel.'

The Doctor shook his head. 'Never heard of them.'

'That doesn't surprise me. The code of silence between these fellows is so strict they'd kill their own mothers rather than breach a confidence. The Krauzzen outfit is the most dangerous in Torodon space. It's controlled by this man...'

Another image appeared, displaying a clutch of Torodon emerging from what looked like a conference chamber. All wore lengthy Japanese-type robes, and again had their long white hair tied in topknots. The central figure had a broad, solid physique and an aristocratic bearing. His face was handsome, if rather cruel.

'Xorg Krauzzen,' Zalu said. 'He's ex-military. He may look normal, but much of his body was destroyed in combat. Most of what you see here is synthetic.'

'Go on.'

'That was years ago. Afterwards, Krauzzen became a mercenary soldier and finally a gun-for-hire in the underworld. With his experience, and his right-hand man – a former fellow commando called Zarbotan, who boasted the highest kill-rate in the entire Special Assault Brigade – it wasn't long before he'd taken over the operation and projected it into the premier league. His outfit became synonymous with extreme ruthlessness.

Now he rules the roost. He's almost untouchable, despite regular involvement in murder, extortion, smuggling…'

'No one's untouchable,' the Doctor said. 'You ought to know that.'

'Just to give you an idea what Krauzzen is like, Doctor… One of his most lucrative income streams comes from organising "fun hunts".'

'Why do I get the impression it's going to be more "hunt" and less "fun"?'

'You know Gorgoror, the moon of Zigriz?'

'Of course. Wouldn't recommend it for a holiday though.'

Another image appeared: it showed a tiny, green planetoid suspended against the much larger, eggshell-patterned surface of Zigriz, a gas giant on the farthest point of the Torodon star system. The sight of the menials working the streets of LP9 had already reminded the Doctor about Gorgoror's one-time role as a work camp for convicts; he tried to recall what else he knew about it. It had a breathable atmosphere, and, warmed by its proximity to Zigriz, it had been extensively excavated. But that was in the past. Centuries of heavy industry had ruined the moon's environment, and it was now swept by cataclysmic storms and intensely corrosive acid rain. As far as the Doctor knew, since Gorgoror had been abandoned, about thirty years earlier, it had become a hellish wasteland littered with toxic ruins.

'The old installations that cover Gorgoror are derelict, but they're still accessible,' Zalu said. 'They're connected to each other by miles of tunnels.'

'Why are you telling me this?' the Doctor asked.

'Gorgoror is Krauzzen's new playground. He takes

captives and releases them into these ruins. He then lets loose parties of big-game hunters – bored rich men who have paid for the privilege.'

'Privilege?' Despite everything he'd seen and done in his many lives, the Doctor's hair was suddenly prickling. 'Ah, you mean the privilege of stalking human prey?'

'Any prey that's rational, able to run. Anything that makes a good moving target. It seems mainly to be humans.'

'So, hang on, Zalu…' Fleetingly, the Doctor had trouble keeping his temper. 'You know all about this. And yet you sit in your office, doing nothing?'

'Krauzzen is beyond our reach.'

'Gorgoror is less than half a day's flight from here!'

'It's not a matter of distance. It's a matter of legalities.'

'Legalities?'

'Look… Central Government considers that these crime syndicates have a role to play. To start with they provide recreational activities for our Outer Rim workforce.'

'And I guess, while these gangs are occupied on the Outer Rim, they aren't bothering anyone on the Inner Rim or, heaven forbid, on Torodon itself?'

'That too. Several years ago, Central Government issued a directive that as long as Torodon nationals are not being victimised by these racketeers, law enforcement must leave them be.'

'And does that work for you when you go home in the evening, Zalu?' the Doctor wondered, backing away. 'Because it wouldn't work for me.'

'Doctor, listen…'

'Tell you what. You continue clock-watching, Zalu… Round up the odd drunk, arrest the occasional pickpocket.

I'll go after the *real* criminals.'

'Doctor…'

The Doctor turned to leave, but found his path blocked by a female police officer carrying a curious-looking rifle; blue pulses of light passed up and down its transparent barrel.

'Meet Point-Sergeant Xelos,' Zalu said.

'Ah yes…' The Doctor gave a wry smile. 'The one who watches a lot of telly.'

Sergeant Xelos responded by pushing the rifle into the Doctor's hands.

'I don't use guns,' he said, pushing it back.

'You're going to have to if you want to help your friends,' Zalu said, taking the gun himself, and forcing it into the Doctor's possession. 'There's only one way you're going to get the better of Xorg Krauzzen's organisation.'

'And how's that?' the Doctor asked.

'You've got to join it.'

Chapter
13

Amy was very grateful that she didn't suffer from claustrophobia.

It only occurred to her once she was inside the aluminium crate that she might be in there for some time. At first she was thrown around wildly, then everything went still and she realised that she was on board the transport craft. She tried to push off the lid, only to find that it was held in place by another crate placed on top of it. At this realisation, it was a struggle to fight down panic. But she held her nerve, waiting tensely and quietly, listening to the hum of a high-powered engine. Several hours passed before she heard a *clunk* and felt a vibration. She was a seasoned enough space traveller to recognise when the craft she was riding on had made contact with another. After a short time, there were voices, and more rough handling.

She realised that she was being brought aboard the aforementioned *Ellipsis*, almost certainly to be placed inside a much larger cargo hold. If they pinned the lid down here, it could be days, weeks, maybe months before they opened it again. The first instant they set her down, she knew she'd have to move. The crate then went still, as though left in a corner. Amy pushed against the lid. It lifted a crack and she peered out. As she'd envisioned, she seemed to be on a cargo deck – its metal floor was stacked with boxes, barrels and other metal containers. A spiral stair rose to a catwalk overhead. There was nobody moving. She couldn't hear anyone speaking.

She lifted the lid, and tried to clamber out, but her limbs were cramped and numb. She dropped the lid onto the floor, where it clattered. She fell to a crouch, her gaze darting in all directions. There was still no sign of anybody else. The hold was a tall, vaulted chamber, but long and narrow. She risked standing up and looked down to its far end, where a forklift was scuttling around and several figures were humping items off a conveyor belt. All their backs were to her.

She turned to run.

And found Xaaael standing behind her.

'Well, well,' he said, 'if it isn't the one who wears the trousers in her relationships.'

'Where's Rory?' Amy snapped. 'If you've hurt him…'

'What?' Xaaael chuckled. 'If we've hurt him… *what*?'

Amy had the urge to blurt out that maybe she couldn't do anything, but that she had a friend who would be on his way right now – but it didn't seem like a good idea to warn them in advance about the Doctor. Not that there was any guarantee the Doctor *was* coming. After all, he didn't have the TARDIS.

She eyed the nearest pile of crates. A passage led

behind it, probably connecting with more passages weaving through the stacks of cargo. It was only a metre or so away. If she could just elude this character long enough to…

'Uh-uh!' Xaaael said, producing a handgun from his hip. 'You've noticed that we're not on LP9 any more. The rules regarding ordnance don't apply here. This, for example… This is a photon-pistol. It discharges a mass of minuscule but energised particles, which travel at such velocity that all matter in their path is annihilated.'

Amy knew that he was trying to frighten her. He had her down as a tough cookie, and he was seeking to cow her, to which there was only one response.

'So is this it?' she asked, planting hands on hips. 'I was told you were a top-class criminal. But all I'm seeing is someone who cheats in the gambling hall and points guns at women.'

He aimed the weapon directly at her face. 'It doesn't have to end with pointing.'

'*Xaaael!*' came a voice from overhead.

They glanced up and saw a figure leaning over the catwalk barrier.

'What's happening there?'

'We have a stowaway, my lord,' Xaaael replied.

The other man descended the spiral stair, and approached. He moved lithely, Amy thought – with the grace of a panther. He was wearing black vinyl boots and trousers, but also a shirt of billowing orange silk, fixed around his waist with a crimson sash – it was a vaguely piratical look. His white hair was long, but hung in a neat ponytail. Despite his cobalt eyes and silver skin, he was startlingly handsome. His face was so smooth, so chiselled, so finely featured that it might have been fake.

'A stowaway?' His voice was deep, resonant.

'She slipped aboard my *Raptor-Bird* on LP9,' Xaaael explained.

'And you let her?'

'I've caught her now, haven't I?' Xaaael spoke defiantly, but in the presence of this other man there was noticeably less swagger about him.

'Let's hope she hasn't got twenty more friends you've missed.'

'She's only got one: the human we brought from LP9.'

'I happen to be his wife,' Amy stated.

The newcomer regarded her with interest. 'You should have brought her originally, Xaaael. It would have made a novel twist, a man protecting his wife.'

'I'm right in front of you!' Amy said. 'You can speak *to* me, if you want to.'

But the newcomer continued to speak *about* her, and what he said next chilled her to the marrow. 'Shame to waste her on a routine hunt. We should put her in the one after next. We can advertise more widely, and charge a special rate for a kill of this quality.'

'What are you talking about?' she demanded. 'Why have you brought us here?'

'Save this one till later, Xaaael. But don't put her in the holding cells. I don't want her spoiling. Give her a job.'

'A job, my lord?'

'In the Salon. We can always use another cocktail waitress.'

Xaaael took Amy by the wrist. 'You don't know how lucky you are. But don't get too comfortable. Luck has a habit of running out on the *Ellipsis*.'

'This is one of the old C10 Interceptors,' Zalu said, almost proudly.

He and the Doctor were inside a hangar to the rear of the Police HQ. In front of them sat a large, bat-winged spacecraft. Its sleek shape and the black heatproof tile-work with which several police engineers were carefully covering it, reminded him of the stealth fighters used on Earth.

'They were employed for pursuing gunrunners operating between the Outer Rim and the Inner Rim,' Zalu explained. 'The series was decommissioned half a century ago. But this one's in good condition.'

'Just what I need,' the Doctor said. 'An antique.'

'I'm loaning you this vehicle because Krauzzen probably won't recognise it.'

'Probably?'

Zalu shrugged. 'You can never be totally sure. That's why I'm disguising it.'

Originally, the Interceptor had been white in colour and covered with official markings. The black tiles weren't just to resist the heat of interplanetary travel.

The basic plan was for the Doctor to pilot himself to the *Ellipsis*, and, on arrival, pretend to be a wealthy playboy looking to buy his way into the next 'fun hunt'. The Doctor had no money of course – something which never ceased to amaze Zalu ('How you can get around the average supermarket, never mind the cosmos, without needing to spend cash, is beyond me!'). So a steel briefcase sat at his feet, containing Torodon tender to the tune of three million par-creds, which Zalu's officers had recently confiscated from a gang of conmen working the casinos. The money would, in due course, need to be exhibited for evidence, so it was imperative that the Doctor returned it safely. There was no doubt that so much money would be enough to persuade Krauzzen to make room for him on the next hunt – the going rate was 500,000 par-creds (partly refundable if you brought down sufficient 'game' to impress Krauzzen himself). However, like all criminal gangs, the syndicate were wary of being infiltrated by government agents, and would demand that he prove his credentials. This was where the transmat-rifle – the weapon given to him by Sergeant Xelos – came in.

'This is advanced stuff,' Zalu warned the Doctor, showing him how to prime the surprisingly light weapon. 'In fact, we're still trialling it. This one's a prototype.'

'I've already said, I don't use guns.'

'But Krauzzen and his people do, and if you want them to trust you, you've got to at least be carrying one.'

'I don't like guns.'

'There's nothing in the transmat-rifle to dislike. It was specifically developed to apply non-lethal force.'

Zalu put it to his shoulder, taking aim at one of the techs working on the Interceptor. The tech noticed, but was unconcerned. Zalu indicated the sights, which contained a tiny frame in which a green image of the target was emblazoned.

'Use this electroscopic sight, Doctor, and you can't miss. But any target you hit, though it will look as if it's been disintegrated, will actually have been teleported to a secure police cell here on LP9.' He handed the weapon over. 'Of course, Krauzzen won't know that.'

'Portable transmat technology,' the Doctor replied,

impressed. 'Is the transmat range good for Gorgoror?'

'It's good for the entire Outer Rim,' Zalu said. 'I'd let you test it now, but as I say, it's still in development. It's only capable of delivering three payloads before needing a safety diagnostic. Discharge it after that and it may really disintegrate its targets.'

The Doctor inspected the weapon. It had a folding barrel, and a vinyl strap, by which it could be carried. He slung it over his shoulder then picked up the case of money. 'Well… a-hunting we will go.'

In the cockpit, there were arrays of complex controls. One of Zalu's techs leaned through the open canopy and explained some of the more difficult manoeuvres, only to be surprised at how much the Doctor already knew.

'It's all a bit rushed,' came Zalu's voice through the com-link. 'But I'm afraid time isn't on your side. You're cleared for take-off, so whenever you're ready.'

'I don't often admit this,' the Doctor said, 'but I could still use some help.'

'I'm going out on a limb doing this much for you.'

'That's another reason you were disguising the ship, wasn't it? Deniability?'

Zalu paused, before saying: 'Let's hope it doesn't come to that.'

The Doctor hit various switches, powering up the hyperdrive.

'Remember, Doctor, the transmat-rifle can only be used three times. After that, who knows what'll happen.'

'Like you said,' the Doctor replied, 'let's hope it doesn't come to that.'

Chapter
14

'**Where are we?**' **Sophie** whimpered, clinging to Andrei.

Their captors had herded them into a group, wielding rods with glowing orbs at the end, which Harry had come to think of as 'punch-sticks', given that mere contact with one of those orbs inflicted a severe body blow. A circular hatch slid back, and they were driven along a cylindrical passage made from glowing fabric. As they proceeded, they experienced suction and even weight loss. Soon they were tumbling, unable to stop themselves. At the far end, they crammed into a sealed chamber, before another circular door opened and they were admitted into a spacious area constructed from bare, pewter-coloured metal. The atmosphere and gravity in here were normal, though various tables and chairs had been bolted to the floor. Further doors stood open on small, cubicle-like compartments.

The entry slid closed behind them, and they were alone.

'What is this?' Sophie said again, small-voiced with fear.

'This is the *Ellipsis*,' someone replied. A figure emerged from one of the cubicles. 'A Torodon star-cruiser adapted into a fortified residence.'

The newcomer was youngish with spiky, red hair and a hatchet-nose. He looked pale and drawn, and was wearing a bloodstained bandage around his brow.

Harry looked at him askance. 'Are you saying we're…'

'Don't ask idiot questions like are we in space or have we been abducted by aliens,' the newcomer replied. 'It's surely obvious that's what's happened?'

'Star-cruiser?' Harry's tone suggested the mere idea was ridiculous.

Rory eyed the burly, bearded man in front of him, wondering if he was pretending to be stupid or if this was his natural state.

'Who are *you*?' Andrei asked.

'The name's Rory Williams. I'm a prisoner. Just like you.'

'Why've they taken us?' Dora demanded.

Rory shrugged, focusing on Andrei, and noting that he and several others had rucksacks with them. 'You people look like you were *expecting* to travel?'

'We were expecting to travel to the UK,' Andrei explained. 'To find work.'

Rory rubbed his chin. 'So that's how they've been doing it.'

'Doing what?' Harry asked.

Before Rory could answer, there was a pneumatic *hisss*, and a section of ceiling lowered itself. Three

Torodon, including the semi-mechanical giant, Zarbotan, were standing on it. He carried a massive Perspex trough filled with a sludgy grey paste. The other two Torodon were carrying punch-sticks. The elevator-pad touched down and everyone flocked towards it, demanding explanations.

'Silence!' Zarbotan boomed in his bell-like voice. 'Your questions will be answered in due course. In the meantime, eat!'

He dumped the trough on a central table. Up close, the grey sludge looked even more revolting.

'What is this stuff?' Harry asked.

'Synthetic protein,' Zarbotan replied.

'Synthetic!' Sophie said, backing away. 'I only eat organic.'

Zarbotan was indifferent. 'It's your choice. But it will give you energy, and energy is something you'll soon need.' He turned back to the elevator-pad.

'Hey!' Harry said. 'You don't need my wife and daughter. I'm the one who messed up. Take me. Surely that'll solve this problem?' Zarbotan ignored him. Harry ran after him, clamping a hand to his shoulder. 'Damn it, listen to me!'

Zarbotan spun around with a speed that belied his massive bulk, and jabbed Harry in the belly with a punch-stick. There was a flash and crackle, and Harry was hurled backwards, landing on the rugged metal floor as if he'd been kicked by a horse.

'I also advise that you take no action necessitating reprisals,' Zarbotan said. 'You will soon require the full integrity of your bodies. Eat! You have five minutes.'

'Until what?' Dora demanded, kneeling beside her

groaning husband.

Zarbotan didn't reply. He and his sidekicks stepped onto the elevator-pad, and it re-ascended.

'H-hey!' Harry stammered groggily. 'You… can't leave us…' He struggled back to his feet, but their captors were already out of reach.

Rory watched as the pad vanished through the ceiling, slotting so perfectly into the oval aperture that a join was scarcely visible. He turned to the table. 'We should do as he said and try to eat something.'

'I'm not eating that slop,' Harry replied.

'Up to you, mate,' Rory said, sticking a fingertip in to test the temperature, and, finding it lukewarm, raising a globule to his probing tongue. It didn't just look like mulched paper, it tasted like it. Grimacing, he selected one of several plastic drinking-tubes which had been inserted into the porridge around the edges of the trough. 'But think of it this way… if they were planning to kill us, they'd hardly be feeding us.'

This made sense to Andrei, who beckoned his friends forward. Even Sophie forgot her principled stand against non-organic sustenance when the strong, handsome stranger who'd become her latest rock indicated that it might be a good idea.

Soon only Harry stood away from the trough. 'I said I'm not eating that slop.'

'Oh, for heaven's sake, Harry!' Dora snapped, cringing as she swallowed the vile muck. 'Why should these people want to poison us? Come and have some – you don't know when you'll get a chance to eat again. If nothing else, we should play along. You know that's always best in hostage/captor situations.'

'If we're hostages,' Harry said, 'and they think they're going to get some kind of ransom for us, good luck to them.'

He eyed the sorry bunch Andrei had with him: there were five in total, ranging from the teenaged to the middle-aged. They looked tired, frightened and bedraggled. Their clothes were stained and dirty, their cheeks streaked with tears.

'Even all of us together, I don't think we're worth very much,' he added.

'That depends on who's paying,' Rory replied. 'They didn't go to this trouble for nothing. I reckon we're worth a tidy sum to somebody.'

Chapter
15

Amy was surprised to find most of the interior of the *Ellipsis* plush and comfortable, more like an ocean liner than a battle-scarred spacecraft manned by desperadoes. Its galleries, companionways and stairwells were richly carpeted and wood-panelled, and decorated at regular intervals by large, exotic plants, which sprouted from loam-filled stone pots, the vines of which were allowed to grow all across the walls and ceilings; at the end of these, curled flowers gave off changing patterns of luminous colour. For this reason no artificial light was needed, at least not in the communal areas.

Every so often she encountered gangs of Torodon ruffians lounging on its balconies, or draped across the divans in its lounges. Some were wearing maintenance clothing, but the majority were in that voluminous silken comfort-garb – the Japanese style apparel that she'd seen Xaaael sporting on LP9. It appeared to be the fashion among these mobsters to fasten their white hair tightly

– either in a ponytail or topknot, but here, on their home base, they let it loose. Many manes were extremely long and lustrous. Shimmering white locks hung almost to the smalls of their backs. Amy was reminded of the samurai culture on Earth.

There were plenty of Torodon females on board too, but virtually all were in a servant capacity, either cleaning or scurrying about as waitresses.

This was to be Amy's future, Xaaael said, as he led her into what he called 'the Salon', a spacious lounge, filled with sofas and divans, and hanging screens onto which popular entertainments from Torodon – everything from bizarre sports to what looked like movies – were being beamed. At one side, there was a raised area, possibly for live entertainment, while the other was occupied by an extensive bar counter, which curved around one edge of the Salon for maybe a hundred metres, and was operated exclusively by female barkeeps. Close beside this was a panoramic viewing port, though it didn't show the vastness of space; rather, it was filled by the curved outline of a planet whose surface appeared to be hidden beneath streamers of drifting cloud – most of them yellow or greenish grey; they looked more like scummy suds on the surface of a pond polluted with filth. To complete the illusion, occasional dollops of blackness were submerged below the outer layers of atmosphere like nightmare life forms lurking in a poisoned sea. Amy couldn't imagine what these were, but from the *Ellipsis*'s proximity to the planet, she suspected it was in low orbit, and so wondered if they might be colossal storms – tornados or hurricanes, which had sucked up vast quantities of rubble and debris from the planet surface.

More Torodon males littered the room. However, one smaller group were slightly different. Firstly, they wore very distinctive clothing – a kind of paramilitary battle garb, but in newish, near-pristine condition, rather than worn and patched like the armour worn by the gangsters. Secondly, they were keeping themselves to themselves. There were five of them, and they were holding court in one corner of the Salon, where they drank and laughed together, and moved pointers around a chequerboard marble surface, which Amy suspected was another Torodon way of placing bets. One of them happened to glance in her direction, and she was surprised to recognise him. He was tall and lean, and his outfit was patterned with black and grey tiger stripes, but his face was definitely familiar. It was the Torodon entertainer, Zubedai, who she'd seen down on LP9, though his outrageous afro was absent. Presumably that was a wig, because now he sported a cranium shaved bare except for a small Mohawk strip.

'Those guests are no interest to you,' Xaaael said, tightening his grip on Amy's wrist and hauling her across the room. 'Time to meet to Madam Xagra.'

Another of the guests now saw her, however, and crossed the Salon to intercept them. 'What's this?' he said with interest.

He had a squat, muscular frame and wore a suit of jet-black vinyl. His head was large and squarish, and perched on a powerful neck. His white Torodon locks were sheared down to bristles, and his face covered in scars.

'A new domestic, Colonel,' Xaaael replied. 'Nothing to get excited about.'

The 'Colonel' regarded Amy the way he would a hearty meal. 'Seems a shame to waste an Earthling on domestic chores. We'd get great sport chasing a handsome specimen like this across the surface of Gorgoror.'

'Perhaps,' Xaaael said, leading Amy on. 'But not yet.'

'I'll pay extra for the opportunity.'

'That's the idea,' Xaaael said over his shoulder, to roars of laughter.

Amy was taken behind the bar counter and along a narrow passage into a small room cluttered with computer terminals. In here, her hands bouncing from one keyboard to the next, her eyes flicking from screen to screen, was the aforementioned Madam Xagra. When they entered, she stood up – and was without doubt the largest female Amy had ever seen. She was almost two metres tall, with broad shoulders and a stocky, manlike physique. She wore a long, shapeless garment cinched at the waist, with its sleeves rolled back to the elbows, revealing fat forearms covered with bangles, and podgy, silver fingers decked with jewel-encrusted rings. Her voluminous white hair was piled on top of her head like a Restoration-era wig, and fixed in place with steel pins. She wore as much vivid make-up as any of the other Torodon women, but she was neither handsome nor attractive. She had a broad, flat nose, eyes that were too far apart, an apelike mouth and a protruding lower jaw.

'Well,' she said, after Xaaael had explained things. Her tone implied deep dissatisfaction, as she appraised Amy. 'You're pretty enough in an ordinary, unappealing sort of way. But the first thing we'll have to do is get you dressed appropriately, and have your hair coiffed so that it's the way our men like it.'

Amy was stung, but sufficiently intimidated to keep a lid on it.

'My name is Xagra,' Xagra said, once Xaaael had left them. 'I'm head housekeeper here on the *Ellipsis*. I have two rules. One, my female staff will serve this ship to the fullest extent possible, with both their minds and their bodies. Two, they will obey my every single command as though their life depended on it, which it probably will. Now, my dear… I'm guessing you're here because your family either owes money or some kind of service to Lord Krauzzen?'

'I'm—' Amy began, but Xagra interrupted her.

'I'm not interested. We all have sad pasts here. Yours won't make a jot of difference to me. Until such time as your debts are paid, you are Lord Krauzzen's property and he may do with you as he wishes. Don't be taken in by the polite face he showed you when you arrived. And don't be taken in by mine either.'

If these were their polite faces, Amy wondered how they would respond if she gave them something to complain about.

'Remember, we have life and death control over you,' Xagra added. 'And if the situation requires, we will have no hesitation in imposing the ultimate penalty. Do you understand me, girl?'

Amy nodded, doing her best to maintain the frightened rabbit act – though it wasn't too difficult.

'Good,' Xagra said. She leaned across the room, and hit a button. 'I shall summon one of the other girls, to show you the basics. However, I expect all my staff to be fully conversant with their role here within half a day of their recruitment—'

'May I ask one question?' Amy said.

Xagra looked at her askance. 'Excuse me?'

'Ma'am!' Amy hastily added. 'May I ask one question, ma'am.'

Xagra still looked dazed by such unexpected impudence. 'If you must.'

'What is that dreadful-looking planet we're orbiting?' Amy nodded through the room's single porthole.

'Ah,' Xagra's brutish features formed a rictus grin beneath her garish, pancaked make-up. 'That is the moon of the planet Zigriz. We call it Gorgoror. It is worth you knowing about that place, actually, if for no other reason than to inform you that there are far worse fates than a lifetime's servitude on the *Ellipsis*.'

Chapter

16

The descent was terrifying.

With plasma rockets blazing behind them, they were moving faster than freefall, arrowing downward in a near-vertical trajectory. Each of the prisoners was manacled hand and foot to his or her own upright pillar in the rear section of the drop-ship. Rory was positioned so as to be facing through the hatchway connecting with the pilot's compartment, inside of which Zarbotan and two other Torodon gangsters lazed on benches, checking and priming pistols and rifles. A fourth sat at the controls.

'You'll feel a little gravity sickness when we first touch down,' Zarbotan had said while they were being chained. 'It will pass shortly.'

Harry had tugged futilely at his shackles. 'Damn it, where are you taking us?'

Zarbotan had looked him in the eye long and hard before replying: 'Gorgoror.'

Gorgoror.

That was the name of the moon they were now hurtling towards. Even before they punched through its atmosphere, it had a hellish aspect: layer upon layer of cloud and toxic vapour, which spattered the craft's outside lenses with greasy, grainy fluid – as though filled with char or ash. But once this smog rolled back, a true Stygian realm was revealed. Rory craned his neck, to see past the pilot's head. A barren wasteland met his eyes: a ruined, blighted landscape, striated with ridges of crags so sharp were they like rows of serrated teeth – and all lashed by rain and howling wind. In fact, the winds were of phenomenal strength; even at high altitude, the dropship was buffeted as it descended, setting the prisoners gasping and groaning in their chains.

Without warning, they pulled straight out of their headlong dive and hit the horizontal. Suddenly Rory had a better view of what awaited them. A series of transparent domes passed by below. They were similar in shape and size to the dome that covered LP9, yet these were stained and filthy, and in many places broken. The craft skimmed closely over the top of them – so close that he could see cluttered buildings underneath, begrimed with smoke or soot. Many were shattered, just gutted shells, the wastelands between them strewn with rubble and wreckage.

Harry was chained with his back to the pilot's compartment, so he saw none of this, but he had a clear view of Rory's face, which had paled.

'What is it?' Harry shouted.

Rory shook his head. He couldn't give voice to the fear gnawing at his guts.

A split second later, those guts almost spilled when

the craft flipped itself over and made another precipitous downward plunge. The rest of the prisoners shrieked.

Rory screwed his eyes shut as they descended in a tailspin. Then – again with no warning – the craft inverted itself. The next thing Rory knew, they were hovering. There was an ear-punishing throb from the retro-rockets.

He glanced again into the pilot's compartment. The view-screen had turned itself off, and the pilot was no longer at the controls. Clearly, they were being guided in by a computer. When they landed, it was almost gentle.

Zarbotan and his associates barged through into the rear section. They were all wearing similar clothing: all-in-one hooded coveralls, harnessed tightly and made from some rubbery, two-tone material. They pulled on gauntlet gloves stained with oil and other dark substances, before unfastening the prisoners' manacles. There was a ghastly prolonged squeal – the sound of hydraulics so arthritic that they surely needed replacing – as the drop-ship's rear ramp swung downward. A numbing cold seeped in, and there was a stomach-churning stench: sulphur, chlorine and other foul chemicals. Just breathing it made the nose and throat raw.

'Outside!' Zarbotan bellowed. 'All of you!'

They complied wearily, too nauseated to argue – and too aware of the rifles trained on them. At the foot of the ramp, they saw that they were enclosed in a vast but empty building. Black brick walls, running with moisture, rose into infinite darkness. A shockingly bright arc-light sprang to life on their left, but it only illuminated the area where they were standing: a circular steel landing-pad, its surface badly charred. They blinked and shivered, huddled together amid plumes of their own smoky breath.

Zarbotan strode to a vertical ladder, which dropped into darkness. 'Follow me.'

They complied, his men bringing up the rear. Halfway down, they could have stepped off onto a separate catwalk, which led away into shadow, but Zarbotan ignored this and proceeded to the very bottom, where he switched on a flashlight embedded in his harness. The glow revealed a floor of impacted mud.

'This way,' he said, striding off.

Nervously, struggling to keep their footing, the prisoners followed. Sophie cried out as she tripped, landing in a pool of liquid muck, which plastered the front of her dress, and coated her hands and face. Dora tried to help, but Sophie shrugged her off, leaving the honour to Andrei.

'What is this place, do you think?' Harry wondered quietly.

Rory shook his head. All around them were junked industrial relics: ancient machinery, fallen girders. 'I don't think it's anything any more,' he said.

'Hurry up!' Zarbotan shouted back. 'We're not here at your convenience.'

'Let's take them?' Harry suggested.

Rory shook his head. 'I think we should play along.'

'It's dark in here. They probably can't see any better than us.'

'They're armed.'

'Yes, but there are more of us than them. We'd have the advantage.'

Rory grabbed him by the collar. 'You're going to get us all killed. Why don't you stop playing the big man, and let's see how this pans out!'

Harry pulled free, muttering something hostile, but he continued forward, and made no attempt to do anything else.

Zarbotan led them through a pair of large, folding metal doors now jammed on their corroded tracks, beyond which lay open ground. At least here they had better vision, thanks to weak daylight filtering through the roof of the dome. Several metres to their right, fluid trickled downward in a glinting shaft. The pool into which it was falling bubbled and steamed. The ground was covered by a crust of ash and cinders, which crunched and gave when they trod on it. The colossal heap of brick and rotted steel from which they had just emerged looked like the exhaust tower to some gigantic and now abandoned underground facility. In every other direction the gaunt ruins of similar buildings lowered.

'Go ahead!' Zarbotan said.

Sophie was halfway towards the pool of water.

'Go ahead,' he said again, but something in the way he said it stopped her in her tracks. Filthy and humiliated though she was, she regarded him uncertainly. 'Wash yourself in *that*,' he added, 'and see what happens.'

With his half-dead face and semi-mechanical voice, it was impossible to tell whether or not he was being serious. The other captors looked amused. Sophie retreated towards Andrei, who put a protective arm around her.

Zarbotan scooped up a discarded tool, a combination of spade and pickaxe, walked towards the pool and threw it in. The prisoners watched agog as the steel implement dissolved like butter, melting away in thick twists of pungent smoke.

He turned to face them. 'You're advised, during your stay here, not to go outside these domes. There are seven in total – they cover a petrochemical plant, a nuclear power station, a munitions factory, a sulphur mine with an attached labour camp, a toxic waste refinery and a spaceport. All are derelict and lie miles apart from each other across the exposed surface of this moon. But it's possible to move between them underground, where there are connecting tunnels and galleries—'

'Wait!' Harry interrupted. 'What do you mean "during our stay here"?'

Zarbotan regarded him blankly. 'What do you think? We've brought you here for a vacation.'

The other criminals sniggered.

'You can't just maroon us here!'

'It won't be for long,' Zarbotan replied.

'How long? Tell us, please.'

'In most cases no more than a couple of days.'

Harry almost looked relieved. 'I... don't suppose that's too bad.'

The other criminals openly laughed. Even Zarbotan cracked a half-smile.

'At least tell us how we can get food and water,' Andrei said.

'You must scavenge. That's what everything else down here does.'

'Everything else?'

Zarbotan smiled – again it only affected half of his mouth. 'My friend, you'll be so busy trying to avoid becoming food yourself that you won't have time to worry about eating.'

More laughter broke from the rest of the gang.

Suddenly Rory couldn't stand it any longer. 'Why don't you just quit this stupid game!' he said. 'These brainless hyenas may laugh at your every word because they're scared to death of you. But that's as far as it goes. So let's stop pretending, eh? You're going to tell us why we're here at some point. Why not get on with it?'

Zarbotan fixed his soulless eyes on Rory. 'As I told you, there are seven areas in this Chase.'

'Chase?' Such a simple word, yet Rory felt as if it realised all his worst fears.

'Use them well, and live,' Zarbotan added. 'For a time.'

The criminals now shouldered their firearms, and trooped back towards the exhaust-tower. The prisoners watched in frozen silence. None of the gang looked back. Not even Zarbotan.

'Well done!' Harry said under his breath. He rounded on Rory. 'Well done, pal! Let's play along, you said! Let's see how it pans out! Are you happy now?'

'At least you're alive,' Rory retorted.

'Yeah, but for how long?'

There was a grinding roar as, one by one, the dropship's propulsion jets were fired, each amplified by the interior of the vast, hollow building.

Rory shook his head. 'Looks like that'll be up to us.'

Chapter
17

'My lord, we have a late entrant for tomorrow's hunt.'

The electronic voice issued from the Bridge computer. It echoed across the Salon via intercom. Amy glanced up – she was in the process of clearing empty beakers from a table top. As Xagra had threatened, they'd changed her appearance to suit the Torodon style. They'd spiked her hair and filled it with rainbow colours, and had given her a skintight cat-suit to wear, which she thought rather fetching. Not that anybody in the Salon appeared to be noticing her now – not even the one called Colonel, who'd shown such unhealthy interest in her earlier.

He and the other group she'd seen gambling were now being entertained by Krauzzen personally. He too was placing counters on the chequerboard marble. By the sounds of the conversation, he was discussing the odds for the following day's big event – whatever that was going to be.

'My lord...?' the computer voice said again.

'Yes, yes,' Krauzzen replied without interest. 'A late entrant. How unfortunate. All the slots are filled.'

'I've told him that, lord. But he says he will pay a tidy sum.'

'They all pay a tidy sum.'

Krauzzen's guests laughed.

'This one is quite keen. He's outside now.'

Krauzzen looked up. 'Outside?'

'He's made his own way here.'

Amy managed to suppress a surge of hope and continued to gather the empties.

'Indeed,' Krauzzen said. 'Tell him that if he wishes to join the next hunt, he may, but only by approaching through correct channels. Remind him we have booking agents on all the main leisure platforms. Remind him as well that we don't take kindly to direct approaches of this nature. If he doesn't vacate *Ellipsis* space forthwith, we'll be forced to defend ourselves – and blow him and his craft to atoms.'

'My lord, he insists on joining the hunt.'

'*Insists?*'

Amy's heart was thudding. She placed her tray down and began to rearrange it – anything to delay having to vacate the Salon.

'He says he will pay double the normal entry fee,' the computer explained.

'Who is he?'

'He calls himself "the Doctor".'

Amy had to bite her lip.

Krauzzen glanced around at his guests, none of whom seemed any wiser. 'Patch him through.' He turned to one of the hanging screens.

The previous image was scrambled and a new one appeared. Amy almost laughed aloud at the grinning face and floppy mass of unruly hair.

'Lord Krauzzen?' the Doctor said. By the gadgetry crammed around him, he was in a spacecraft command chair, though his boots were up on the control block, and he held a crystal flute filled with what looked like champagne.

'Who are you?' Krauzzen asked.

The Doctor gave this some thought, before replying: 'I'm the deadliest hunter on the Outer Rim.'

'Are you? How impressive.'

'Very impressive, I think. Or was that not a question? Sorry.'

Krauzzen's guests exchanged amused glances. Amy saw Xaaael enter the Salon. He'd clearly overheard the conversation on the intercom. He approached, intrigued.

'Whoever you really are, Doctor, you're clearly a fool,' Krauzzen said. 'That much is obvious, merely from looking at you. But to call yourself the deadliest hunter on the Outer Rim... I have some of our highest-scoring clients with me now. And none of them have ever heard of you.'

'Well, you can hardly hold me responsible for their shortcomings, can you?'

'But I can for your own. Might I advise that you now clear the vicinity of this vessel! Before I order my starboard batteries to do it for me.'

Krauzzen turned from the screen.

'So it's true what they say about you, then,' the Doctor shouted. 'That your hunts are fixed.'

'Fixed?' Krauzzen twirled back to face him.

'Fixed. Engineered. That your select band of shooters is actually a clique of bumbling amateurs, who come to you to have their egos massaged.'

Krauzzen's guests leaped to their feet, spluttering. The marble board crashed to the Salon floor.

The Doctor laughed. 'Afraid of a little *real* competition? Well, I guess that's understandable.'

'You're quite a speaker,' Krauzzen said, remaining calm despite his obvious fury.

'I'm quite a marksman too.' The Doctor leaned towards the screen. 'I bet that I can finish this hunt with a scorecard three times higher than anyone else.'

There was an amazed silence in the Salon.

'And how *much* are you prepared to wager?' Krauzzen wondered.

'Well… let's see. Your normal rule is that the winner of each hunt, as well as claiming the prize, which is a quarter of each player's entry fee, will also be refunded half his own fee. So, when I win, as well as awarding me the winning pot, you can refund my entire fee.'

'And if you don't win?'

'I'll pay you the same amount again, and a similar amount to the actual winner.'

'Let him come aboard, my lord!' one of the other hunters cried. 'This boy needs a lesson in humility!'

'We'll take him for every penny he has!' another shouted.

'You must be carrying an awful lot of cash,' Krauzzen said.

The Doctor lifted the steel briefcase into view, and opened it, revealing wads of crisp new Torodon par-creds, bound with metallic ribbons.

Amy watched Krauzzen's face. He remained cool, superficially unruffled, but she could tell straightaway that he was hooked. It was ironic, of course. The Doctor was never motivated by money, but there were some for whom there was no other motivation – even to the point where it led them to risk everything they had.

The hunters also fell silent. They stared glassy-eyed at the screen.

'What's to stop us simply taking it from you?' Krauzzen asked.

The Doctor snapped the case closed. 'Oh, credit me with some intelligence. I haven't come here on spec. I've got friends on LP9 and other leisure platforms, including legal advisers. They're all well aware of my plans, and if I simply disappear, it won't take long for the story to get around that *you* can't be trusted and that your "fun hunts" are a farce.'

Amy waited nervously, wondering if the Doctor was taking his brinkmanship a little too far. Men like Krauzzen did not rule their worlds unless they were totally merciless to their opponents. And yet could the crime boss afford to have his reputation tarnished?

'So?' the Doctor persisted. 'Can I come aboard?'

'Do you have a written reference for me, Doctor? No one may join the hunt without a written reference from a former client.'

The Doctor held a leather wallet to the camera and opened it. Krauzzen gazed at the document, puzzled.

'Xandor Konzalar? He was champion of the hunt many times. But he died several years ago. How has it taken you so long to come to us?'

'I've been busy, making money.' The Doctor pocketed

his psychic paper. 'I'm as much a predator in the boardroom as I am on safari.' He gave a little snarl. 'OK, still working on that. But you get the idea.'

Xaaael leaned towards his master's ear. 'If Konzalar vouched for this fellow…'

Krauzzen waved him to silence, before turning to the rest of his clients. 'It's your call, gentlemen. If this contestant is as good as he says he is, you will have to up your game to have a chance of winning tomorrow.'

'Let him come aboard,' Colonel Krelbin replied. 'I always relish a challenge.'

One by one, the others grunted their acknowledgement. They might not have liked it, but with prize money of this sort at stake, it was not an opportunity to miss.

'Permission granted, Doctor,' Krauzzen said. 'There are empty docking bays on the port side of the vessel.'

The Doctor smiled, and cut the communication.

Krauzzen took Xaaael to one side. 'LP9 is your responsibility. Did you see this fellow when you were last down there?'

'Humanoids are not too common out here,' Xaaael said. 'I'd have noticed him.'

'He wasn't with these other Earthlings you brought here?'

'Definitely not.'

Krauzzen paused to think. 'Then we extend him the usual courtesy. Whoever he is, he's clearly a rich bird. We don't want to frighten him away before we pluck his plumage.'

Chapter
18

Unnerved by the blighted landscape around them, Rory and the other prisoners' initial response was to camp close to the spot where they had been dumped, right alongside the exhaust tower, though the drop-ship had long flown from the top of this, drawing a green plasma flare behind it. Once the ship had departed, the aura of their new desolate environment seemed even bleaker. The cold felt colder. The stench of chemical decay intensified. It wasn't even possible to say that their eyes had adjusted to the feeble daylight, because it was actually more like twilight, a deep 'undersea' gloom to which human eyes could never adjust.

Harry was still trying to take charge, but the others were increasingly unresponsive to him, and it was plain to Rory that Harry himself didn't realise just how out of his depth he was. Everyone had accepted that they'd been abducted by aliens, but Harry was under the impression that, at the worst, this was a short-term deal and that in two days their captors would return for them, as they had supposedly promised.

'They never promised any such thing,' Rory said, exasperated.

'Look,' Harry retorted, 'what would be the point in abandoning us here? They must have something else in mind.'

Rory had no doubt about that, but didn't see grounds for optimism in it.

'The other thing is,' Harry said, 'they're obviously more technologically advanced than we are.'

'So?'

'So the more advanced you are, the more civilised you are.'

'You're an ex-cop, did you say?'

'That's right.'

'Forgive me for saying this, but you seem a bit naive.'

'Hey!' Harry's smile faded. 'Maybe I can just see the good in people?'

Rory almost gave up talking to him at that point, but resisted the temptation to walk away. If nothing else, they had to stick together for safety and work as a team.

The first thing they did was cast around for pieces of rubbish with which to make a fire. They finally got a small blaze going, which wouldn't last long. Rory surveyed the scene as the small group huddled around the flames. It was like the worst kind of squatter camp: wasteland on all sides, everyone ragged and hungry. He'd now got to know the rest of his companions. Harry was here with his wife and daughter, Dora and Sophie, though in some ways he was estranged from them, particularly Sophie, who was currently clinging to this other guy, Andrei.

Andrei appeared to be the spokesman for the other half of the group. This included two Albanian brothers called Miklos and Grigor; neither of them was more than 20 years old, and neither of them could speak English. The other members comprised an older Iraqi man named Yasin, who was clearly ill, and his younger sister, Rukia, who was university educated and spoke reasonable English, but who was using all her energy and intellect trying to assist and placate her older sibling.

'What are we going to do for food?' Harry asked Rory.

'Has anyone got any food with them?'

Harry shrugged. 'These foreigners apparently brought some, but they've been prisoners for days now and there's nothing left. Zarbotan mentioned there was wildlife, didn't he? Maybe we should set some traps, get some spears together?'

Rory couldn't put into words what he felt about this suggestion. Even on Earth, in the middle of a game reserve, he doubted this worn-out ragbag of humanity could successfully hunt. Here, they didn't even know if the fauna was edible. Glancing at the cindery plain, at the piles of scorched metal, and tors of twisted, tormented rock, it seemed impossible that a fruitful ecosystem could exist. Anything roaming this dreary vista had most likely been imported, and Rory didn't like to imagine why. Before he could give voice to this doubt, there was a long, eerie call from somewhere across the wasteland.

'Look,' Sophie said, standing up and pointing.

Perhaps a hundred metres away, a figure was approaching. Rory squinted, trying to see properly in the gloom. The figure was bipedal, but of heavy build and covered with a shaggy pelt. It cried out again – a ghostly, ululating howl. It was coming towards them, and with increasing speed. What was more, the closer it drew the larger it looked – soon it was the size of a bear. Rory saw clouds of breath issuing from its tusk-filled snout. He saw gleaming green jewels where its eyes should be, a great, curved horn in the middle of its forehead.

'I think we should get out of here,' he said, backing away.

The creature gave another ear-shattering howl.

'Quickly!' Rory shouted. 'Run!'

'Back inside the landing base!' Harry cried.

'No!' Rory argued. 'Those doors are jammed open – it'll corner us in there. *Just run!*'

Chapter
19

'**I thought I knew** every piece of artillery in the galaxy,' Krauzzen said. 'But this is something new.'

The Doctor was standing in the Salon, surrounded by mobsters. 'Lord' Xorg Krauzzen had introduced himself, and was now examining the transmat-rifle.

'It's my own design,' the Doctor explained modestly.

Krauzzen handed the rifle back. His eyes looked real enough, even if they did glint like blades, but his silver face, though superficially smooth and handsome, was so evidently synthetic that no emotion could easily be read from it.

'So you're an inventor as well as a businessman?' Krauzzen posed it as a question, but scepticism was implicit.

'I'm all sorts of things.'

'Well, so long as your money checks out, you can be anything you wish.'

At a table nearby, Xaaael and two others had opened

the briefcase and were counting the Torodon tender into neat piles.

'Of course,' Krauzzen added, 'having an impressive gun is one thing. The question is, can you use it?'

The Doctor tensed; he'd been expecting something like this.

'Xalva!' Krauzzen called, looking to the far side of the Salon, where another of his lackeys – a big, powerful gangster, whose comfortable robes did little to conceal his muscle-packed frame – was standing with arms folded. 'Xalva, you've carried out more hits for me than most this last year. Kill this fellow.'

Xalva looked puzzled. 'My lord?'

'Kill him. He's come here to destroy us, so I want him dead!'

There was a clattering of chairs and tables as those gathered around the Doctor scattered in various directions. Xalva thrust a hand into a holster and pulled out a pistol, priming it and taking aim in one fluid movement. But the Doctor had already put the transmat-rifle to his shoulder, and hit the trigger. A pulse of blue energy crossed the room in a clean, straight line, and struck Xalva dead on. There was a glaring flash, and he vanished.

One of Krauzzen's other henchmen scuttled over. When he returned, all he held in his hand was a pile of charred dust. The Doctor deactivated the rifle, and slung it over his shoulder. The gangsters wouldn't know it, but that dust represented the air molecules in the target's immediate vicinity, carbonised by the transmat flash.

There were awed murmurs.

Krauzzen said nothing as he gazed down at the handful of ash.

The Doctor ran a finger around the inside of his collar. 'Sorry about that. But at least I saved you the cost of the crematorium.'

Krauzzen appraised him coolly. Still he said nothing.

Amy now entered, carrying a tray of drinks. She approached Krauzzen's group. The Doctor regarded her as if she was no one, though her skintight cat-suit and multicoloured hair was a bit of a shock. Likewise, she gave no indication that she knew him. Krauzzen watched their interaction carefully.

The Doctor took a drink from the tray. As Amy moved away, he sipped delicately. That was another test hopefully passed. However, a more difficult one was yet to come. On cue, Xaaael rose to his feet.

'My lord, only a quarter of the money is here.'

Krauzzen turned to the Doctor, who merely shrugged.

'The rest is on my spacecraft, and only I have the combination code to reach it.'

Xaaael approached, looking angry. 'Your lack of trust insults us!'

'No insult is intended, honest,' the Doctor told Krauzzen calmly. 'Trust is great, but it must be earned. I'm sure *you* understand that better than anyone?'

'You're telling us our own business?' Xaaael said, enraged. He drew a weapon from his hip – the Doctor noticed that, like Xalva's, it was a photon-pistol. Others of Krauzzen's crew carried photon-rifles, which must have been obtained originally from the Torodon military. There were few more powerful small arms in this galaxy, and suddenly several were aimed in his direction.

'I hate to say this, Lord Krauzzen,' the Doctor said,

'but if anything happens to me, you'll never be able to force entry to my spacecraft. Its access port has a titanium lock primed with a black-light micro-circuitor.'

There were intakes of breath all around the Salon.

Krauzzen held his tongue, but his eyes glinted eerily.

'Black-light?' Xaaael said, sounding stunned.

'That's right,' the Doctor replied. 'Attempt to enter my craft, attempt to destroy it, even attempt to detach it, and you'll blow a hole in your fuselage the size of eighty city blocks. Which, from your docking bays, would doubtless envelop the lower bows where your fuel cells are located. And they contain, at a conservative estimate, a hundred million gallons of liquid hydrogen? I doubt even a ship the size of the *Ellipsis* could repair itself before everyone on board was sucked to oblivion.'

'And if we don't believe you?' Xaaael whispered.

'Why take that chance when all you have to do is play the game?'

'This is how you seek to make friends with us? By blackmail?'

The Doctor turned back to Krauzzen. His tone became harder, bleaker. 'I'm not in the business of making friends, my lord. And neither are you. I mean no disrespect with these precautions. We are all gamblers. Risk is part of our profession. But we can't be blamed for attempting to stack the odds in our favour.'

Krauzzen regarded the Doctor for silent, ice-cold moments. His face was inscrutable, but his body rigid. Only slowly did it relax again.

'Bravo, Doctor,' he finally said. 'It seems you are a man after my own heart. Your impertinence knows no bounds, but I feel we have more to gain from making your acquaintance than we have to lose. Come, meet your competitors.'

With more than a little relief, the Doctor was led across the Salon. However, the first of the other hunters he was introduced to came as a surprise.

'Xalagon Zubedai,' he said. 'Aren't you an entertainer by trade?'

'That's my public face,' the entertainer replied. 'Privately, I'm a different person.'

'So I see.'

There were four other members of the hunting party, and they were exactly the sort he'd expected to find here: middle-aged Torodon males, rich men jaded by the expensive pleasures they'd lavished on themselves. But for all that, they weren't laggardly or unfit; they looked hungry for action. On their home world, they'd be powerbrokers: tycoons, politicians, captains of industry; men whose day-to-day activities required them to be alpha-dogs, yet who in their leisure time took this quest for dominance to an even higher level. They carried an assortment of weapons: everything from pulse destroyers to pneumatic crossbows loaded with exploding arrows. The most fearsome weapon of all looked, at first glance, like a pump-action shotgun – it was short and blocky, though closer inspection would reveal a high-voltage power pack built into the underside of its gleaming black barrel. Its owner, whose name was Xon Krelbin, though the others referred to him as the Colonel, explained that its function was to strike a target with an ion stream so intensely hot that 'blood will boil, bones shatter and internal organs rupture'.

'I call it "the Eradicator",' he said, his toothy grin

giving his scarred face a demonic countenance.

The Doctor eyed Krelbin carefully. Of them all, he looked by far the most virile. He had a squat, compact physique, a bull-neck and wore his white hair shaved to flat bristles. Everything about him indicated combat experience.

'What do you call your own weapon?' Krelbin asked, eyeing the transmat-rifle with a strange mixture of contempt and jealousy.

'Erm… "the Obliterator",' the Doctor said, unable to think of anything more original.

'The problem with it, of course, is that you can't keep trophies if you disintegrate every target.'

'Oh… I don't bother with trophies.'

Krelbin looked scornful. He rummaged in a kitbag and brought out a garment which looked to be made entirely from ratty, greasy hair. 'This is my hunting cape,' he said proudly. 'It brings me luck. That's why I add to it each time. It's comprised entirely of scalps.'

The Doctor tried to feign indifference to this vile revelation.

'I'm just good with the *knowledge* of my kills,' Zubedai put in. 'I work a tedious schedule, touring the platforms. There are times when I simply have to get away and service my own needs. I don't take trophies either, Doctor, but when I'm too old to do this, I'll have a packet of memories that no-one can ever steal from me.'

'I'm in eminent company,' the Doctor replied.

'It's good you feel that way,' Krauzzen said. 'But remember, these are your rivals and will crush your dreams, if you allow them. You evidently understand our purpose, Doctor, so I won't waste time elaborating, except to say this: there are eight targets in total.'

On the nearest screen, eight head-shots appeared. All portrayed ordinary Earth people, though Rory was among them. Evidently, the pictures had been taken while their subjects were in pain.

'You tortured them?' the Doctor asked, teeth gritted.

'Indirectly,' Krauzzen said. 'These pictures were taken during their descent to Gorgoror. It wasn't comfortable for them. The drop-ship we use for product is an old prison-transporter. There are one or two gravity issues, which is what you're seeing here. Would it bother you if I *had* tortured them?'

The Doctor shrugged. 'It won't be much sport if they're in no fit state to run.'

'The stronger ones will be. But we can't be too picky about our subjects. Earth is a good source for this kind of material, but we can't always get top-of-the-range product.'

'And this *product* is on Gorgoror now?'

'We give them a day before we pursue.'

'So they can acclimatise?'

There were chuckles from the other hunters.

'You might call it that,' Krauzzen said, 'but it's actually more a battle to survive. We've captured predatory beasts from various planets and released them down there.'

'Predatory beasts?'

'Inconsequential species,' Zubedai explained. 'Mere obstacles as far as we're concerned, but a problem for the targets.'

'And if, as a result of these inconsequential species, the targets are dead by the time we get there?' the Doctor wondered.

'It's amazing how often that doesn't happen,' Krauzzen said.

'But Lord Krauzzen, if I've paid to hunt, and there's nothing left alive...'

'That's a risk you take,' Krauzzen interrupted. 'But to put your mind at rest... Bridge, anything happening on Gorgoror?'

'Pursuit in progress, my lord,' the robotic intercom replied.

'A pursuit!' Krauzzen eyed his group with interest. 'And we have ringside seats.'

Chapter
20

On Gorgoror, the fleeing fugitives had found reserves of strength they hadn't previously known. Unfortunately, the raging, bloodthirsty beast in pursuit wasn't tiring either. It was about fifty metres behind them, bounding on all fours to increase its speed, when they reached the next cluster of gutted buildings. They scrambled, gasping, through the first entrance they came to, only to find themselves in a chaotic mesh of fallen girders and blackened timbers. Desperate and breathless, they fought their way through. When the creature entered behind them, it gave a mighty roar and, with Herculean strength, began smashing the impediments aside.

Harry took one glance over his shoulder and he knew they weren't going to make it if they just kept running. Close by, a narrow ramp led upward. 'Dora!' He grabbed her wrist. 'This way!'

She peered up in disbelief. Whatever this ramp was, it looked rickety, unsupported by scaffolding of any sort, and was terrifyingly steep.

'We know this thing can outrun us,' Harry stammered. 'But can it out-climb us?'

'You can't be serious!'

'I'm perfectly serious.' He spun around. 'Sophie, where are you?'

There were too many bodies trying to scramble through and over the beams and rubble, for him to get an immediate fix on his daughter. When she suddenly appeared in front of him: she was white-faced, her hair in disarray, her cheeks still smeared with mud.

'We're going up,' he said, trying to grab her.

'What?'

With another howl, the pursuing beast hurled a girder out of its way. It was so close they could feel the heat from it, could smell its rancid breath.

'I'm not going up there,' Sophie said, yanking her hand free.

'Sophie, you'll do as I tell you!'

She shook her head dumbly. 'You don't know what you're talking about.'

'Sophie!' he pleaded.

'No!' she screamed. 'You're wrong! *You're always wrong!*'

She turned and fled with the others, tripping over a cable protruding from the concrete floor. Harry wanted to lurch after her, to help her. But Andrei did that for him, hauling the girl to her feet and running, both of them vanishing through the fallen wreckage. Fleetingly, Harry wondered if maybe he *had* made another mistake. But it was too late to change his strategy now. The others had gone and only he and Dora were left.

He pushed her towards the foot of the ramp – she objected wildly, struggling with him, crying out her daughter's name. He knew there was no time to argue, and propelled her upward. The ramp was of trellised steel, and rusty and greasy with moisture. They fell constantly, barking their elbows, knees and shins. Dora was still shouting and weeping, even when they were about nine metres up. But now the monster had halted at the foot of the ramp, breathing hoarsely. Clearly it was torn between targets. In the end it opted for the one it felt would be easier – Harry and Dora.

When they realised this, they climbed desperately, Dora as eager as her husband. But the ascent was steepening, and they were already exhausted. When the monster started up, there was a clattering and groaning as metal joints warped and tore.

'We're going to die!' Dora wailed.

'No we're not!'

At twenty-four metres up, they reached a platform with a catwalk leading away, bridging the cavernous interior. Harry tried to drag his wife forward, but again she resisted.

'No!' she squawked. 'That thing will collapse. We'll fall to our deaths!'

The monster clambered up behind them, grunting and groaning from its own efforts. The entire structure now shook.

'This whole thing is going to collapse!' Harry said.

'Look what you've brought us to!' his wife wept.

And then another voice intruded. 'Harry, over here!'

On the far side of the catwalk, Harry saw another ramp ascending and connecting with an aperture in the building's wall. A figure was standing in that aperture, waving frantically. It was Rory.

'Over here!' Rory shouted. 'That bridge will hold! I've just crossed it.'

Harry took Dora by the hand, and they proceeded across. Behind them, the monster reached the platform, and bounded in pursuit.

The flickering screen showed two people struggling up the steep metal ramp, and a third, Rory, scrambling down it to try and assist them. The ramp was so flimsy that it swayed beneath their weight.

'The entertainment in this place never ends,' the Doctor said, biting his lip.

'We have audio and visual censors installed in most sections of the Chase,' Krauzzen replied. 'For the protection of our clients, obviously.'

'Obviously.'

On screen, a fourth figure appeared, a hulking brute covered in coarse black hair, lumbering up the ramp. Briefly, a jutting snout and curved horn were visible. The Doctor recognised it immediately.

'Things aren't looking good for these three,' Krelbin said dispassionately. 'That's a moon-buck from the planet Peladon. They're placid if treated properly, but this one is probably starving.'

'Save yourself,' came a panting voice from the screen. It was the older man, addressing Rory. 'You didn't need to come back for us... Go, run!'

'And this is what we do?' the Doctor said. 'Watch them die? Even though we've paid for the privilege of hunting them ourselves.'

'Sometimes, Doctor, yes.' Krauzzen took a drink from a tray; thankfully, this waitress was not Amy. 'Hopefully their colleagues watch them die as well, and it serves as a salutary lesson that, if nothing else, on Gorgoror they must keep running. Always running. Never stopping.'

Rory had now detached himself from the other two, and climbed back up the last couple of metres of ramp on his own. He vanished into a tunnel mouth, only to reappear pushing a huge wooden crate. The other two humans slid past it, and he pushed it down the ramp. It hadn't gained much speed before it crashed into the moon-buck.

The monster was big enough to ride out the blow, though it had to rear up on two legs and almost overbalanced. As the crate spun down into the dimness, it continued up, only for Rory to send a second crate down towards it, and the bearded man to send a third. The monster reared again, but the second crate was turning end-over-end, and struck it full in the chest. It tottered backwards, its clawed hind-feet struggling to grip the slippery metal. The third crate slammed into its legs and swept them from beneath it. The moon-buck fell heavily down the ramp, before sliding over the side and dropping into the wreckage far below, where a spear of jagged metal pierced its torso, leaving it hanging like a fish on a skewer. Rory and his friends stared down wearily, before hurrying out of sight into the tunnel.

'Poor Aggedor,' the Doctor said under his breath.

'What's that?' Krelbin wondered.

'Just thinking aloud.'

'I take it you're impressed?' Krauzzen said. 'You should be. These scrag-ends of human society, these nobodies who their own civilisation has forgotten, can fight for their lives if they're frightened enough. It won't be easy when you get down there.'

Amy now appeared at the Doctor's shoulder. She ignored him when he glanced at her, and collected the latest round of empties. He handed the last one to her purposely. She didn't acknowledge this. Nor did she acknowledge the tiny fold of paper he'd slipped into the palm of her hand. Only when she was back in the kitchen area, and able to steal away from her fellow waitresses for a second, did she open it up. Inside it was the TARDIS key. There was also a message written in scruffy pencil. It read:

Off to Gorgoror. Find TARDIS. Hugs.

Chapter
21

Amy's quarters could have been worse. She shared a bare metal cabin with four other girls, but all had separate bunks and lockers, and the room was air-conditioned. To her surprise, the other girls were friendly and welcoming, adopting the attitude that they were all in this together and had to make the best of things. By the same token, Madam Xagra's bark turned out to be worse than her bite. She had a fondness for making speeches, but most of the rest of the time she was content to delegate duties while she slouched in the swivel chair in her control capsule, though she maintained a presence in other sections of the ship by use of a 'travelling-eye' – a small golden globe, the size of a tennis ball, which whipped through the air at great speed, and through which she could deliver instructions and reprimands.

The work itself was arduous in that it was repetitive. When they weren't serving in the Salon, they were cleaning. They would move in groups around the endless galleries and companionways, going over the same ground again and again. Amy was teamed with a young Torodon called Xendra, who was as extravagantly made up as all the other girls, but carried it off well. Her hair was an immense spray of green and purple, her lips bright pink, and she wore vivid slashes of vermillion eye-shadow. Her clingy dress was an off-the-shoulder number which ended at mid-thigh, but suited her petite figure. It seemed ludicrous that they were both dressed as if going nightclubbing, and yet spent their time mopping and polishing until their joints ached. But that was the way of life on board the *Ellipsis*.

'Why has an Earthling like you been favoured?' Xendra asked, as they worked.

'Favoured?' Amy replied.

'Normally you'd be on Gorgoror by now.'

'I suspect I will be at some point.'

'How do you come to be on the Outer Rim?'

'A gambling debt, would you believe.'

'There's a familiar story,' Xendra said. 'My father's a gambling man too. He's a rigger on one of the refineries, but anything he earns he gambles. He was on LP6. We all were – it was a family holiday. But father couldn't resist the gaming tables. When he'd lost everything, he borrowed money from one of Lord Krauzzen's loan sharks. Needless to say, there was massive interest attached. I'm now working off what he owes. I think I'll be here for a long time yet.'

'You don't sound very upset,' Amy said.

'It's a woman's place to serve. At least here we get bed and board. There are many worse duties we could have been put to.'

'Xendra, there must be a way to get off this ship.'

'What would be the point? They know who my family are. Even if it was possible for me to run away, they'd re-impose the debt on father. They have all kinds of ways to get what they're owed, trust me.'

Xendra suddenly sensed a presence and got vigorously back to her work. Amy glanced over her shoulder as Xaaael passed them by. He gave her an unpleasant lopsided grin, but he didn't stop to make conversation.

'Watch what you say when *he's* around,' Xendra hissed.

'It's because of *him* that I'm here.'

'He's one of the worst of them. He's Lord Krauzzen's underling, but he hates being subservient to anyone. He'll never rise while Krauzzen runs the syndicate, but he isn't respected enough to stage a revolt on his own. The real downside is that he takes all his frustrations out on us. He's in a good mood at present, but believe me, there are times when he can be a nightmare. You need to be particularly careful because you're not Torodon. There are no laws protecting you.'

An hour later, they were despatched to the spaceship's Engineering section, on one of the lower decks. This was the most functional area that Amy had seen. Catwalks passed through web-works of steel ducts and thick rubber cables, or between banks of exposed circuitry, with only mesh grilles to prevent accidental contact. Here and there were command points, where Torodon engineers stood on raised platforms operating freestanding control terminals. The area smelled strongly of oil and engine grease, though again it had to be spotlessly clean.

They worked the catwalks, using a vacuum cylinder

to suck up dust, but if any fragments proved stubborn, employing a simple dustpan and brush.

'How close are we here to the cargo store?' Amy asked.

Xendra eyed her warily. 'You're not still thinking of escaping?'

'I have some property I'd like to retrieve.'

'We menials have no access to the cargo store. Ever.'

'Why not?'

'Why do you think? It's full of contraband and stolen goods. Personally, I'm glad it's locked. If one of us was caught pilfering, I don't like to think what might happen.'

'Xendra, this is nonsense. I saw the cargo store when I arrived here. There were no locked doors. There was no security, nothing.'

'You saw the storage section of the loading bay. Your goods will have been moved to the Secure Hold by now.'

'How do I reach the Secure Hold?'

'It's not too far from here. It's close to the repair shops, down a long green passage. But you'll never get into it. It has a single door so strong that an army couldn't break through. Most of Lord Krauzzen's men have no access either. He trusts them even less than us.'

'Someone must be able to get in there?'

'His senior officers can. Xaaael, for one.'

'I see.'

Xendra suddenly looked scared. 'What are you planning now?'

'Lord Xaaael likes me. He smiles whenever he passes me.'

'Don't be foolish. He smiles because he knows he can

do anything he wants to you. And some day he might.'

'I'll take that chance.'

'No property could be worth such a risk.'

'*This* property is.' Amy took Xendra's hand in hers – it was trembling, so she gripped it tightly. 'If I can retrieve this item, Xendra, it will solve all our problems.'

Chapter
22

There was an air of excitement as the hunters, now fully kitted out, gathered in the boarding area. Attached to Colonel Krelbin's belt was the deadliest-looking knife the Doctor had ever seen – the length and breadth of a machete, but razor-edged and tapered at its tip to a vicious point. No doubt this was the tool with which he'd assembled the components of the hunting-cape he was now wearing.

'May the best man win!' Zubedai said, offering sips from his hipflask.

His tiger-striped fatigues had been complemented by an open-faced helmet with a black visor, and a breathing mask attached to an oxygen cylinder on his back.

Before anyone could respond to this toast, Krauzzen arrived with eight of his henchmen. All wore hooded coveralls, tightly harnessed and made from greenish, rubbery material.

'Zarbotan, you're in charge here,' Krauzzen said to someone the Doctor hadn't seen until now, though he remembered the name. The newcomer stood more than two metres tall, and his hard, angular shape implied that he was at least partly mechanical. But his face was his most macabre feature. It looked to have been patched together from the fragments of two other faces. 'I'll be operating the Observation Booth,' Krauzzen told him. 'Maintain full communications. But if anyone gives you a problem, you have my permission to deal with them as you see fit.'

The disfigured giant nodded.

Krauzzen turned to the rest of them. 'After you, gentlemen.'

Compared to the drop-ship reserved for 'product', the drop-ship for the hunting party was the last word in comfort. It was spacious and airy, and contained restful, reclining seats. There was even a bar area, and two waitresses on hand to provide a stewardess service. Through one of several viewing ports, the Doctor was able to assess the *Ellipsis* as they tilted away from it. It was huge of course, and in shape was curved like a crescent moon lying flat. But it was burned and scarred all over, as if it had seen many battles. Plenty of exterior weaponry was visible, while numerous shuttle, transport and fighter craft, minute in comparison, were clustered along its many docking ports. The *Ellipsis* itself was dwarfed by Zigriz, the eggshell-coloured gas giant lowering behind it, blotting out most of space.

'Enjoying the view?' Krauzzen asked.

'The Outer Rim has many wonders,' the Doctor replied. 'It's no surprise you make this your home.'

'*Temporary* home,' Krauzzen corrected him. 'The *Ellipsis* has been in orbit around Gorgoror for several years, but our interstellar thrust is in perfect order. There may come a time when I feel the urge to move on.'

'Not too soon though, eh?' one of the others shouted. 'The Colonel may dominate the scoring at present, but I've a mind to wrest that title from him in due course.'

'You'll have plenty opportunities yet, Krillig,' Krauzzen replied.

Descending through Gorgoror's turbulent atmosphere, a furious storm buffeted the craft, and each passenger was forced to belt himself in. At last, however, they slipped through a crevice in the roof of one of the planetoid's vast domes, and entered a massive black-brick structure. They disembarked onto a landing pad scarred by retro-rocket bursts. By the glare of a powerful arc-light, they climbed down a vertical ladder, stepping onto a separate catwalk, which led to a closed slide-door. Krauzzen tapped in a combination, and the door slid open revealing a snug interior, crammed with monitors and other instrumentation, but warm and lit by a dull, reddish light. Once inside, Krauzzen's men relaxed, pulling up chairs and commencing work on various control panels. The hunting party primed their weapons.

'The last word from the Bridge, gentlemen, is that all eight targets are alive,' Krauzzen said. 'Though they have split into two groups, one of which has been sighted near the prison. The other is headed for the power plant.'

'Hardly seems sporting,' the Doctor said. 'A heads-up like this.'

'The Gorgoror Chase covers hundreds of square-miles,' Krauzzen replied. 'I haven't an infinite amount of spare time on my hands, even if you have. Speaking of which, as this is your first time here –' He took something from a locker; it looked like a space helmet – 'I'd advise you to wear this vision-helm. You can call a variety of charts and maps onto the inside of the visor.'

The Doctor waved the item away. 'I studied the schematics on board the *Ellipsis* last night. I won't need this.'

'Are you mad?' Zubedai asked him.

'No one else is wearing one.'

'Because they don't need to,' Krauzzen said. 'They've been here many times.'

'That gives them an advantage,' the Doctor admitted. 'But my superior skills give me one. It all balances out in the end.'

'You're possessed of soaring confidence, Doctor,' Krelbin sneered. 'I'll say that for you. I see you're not even wearing protective clothing.'

'That would slow me down, and I prize my agility. Mr Agile – that's me.'

'If you do find you run into trouble,' Krauzzen said, 'remember that we have eyes and ears all over the complex. You need only shout. In truth, you may not even need to do that. You'll never know when we might be watching you.'

Chapter
23

The creature was composed entirely of viscous, translucent ooze.

Its body reared up in front of them – if it could really be called a body – so that it filled the entire subterranean passage. It was little more in truth than a shapeless, malleable blob, but it had a revolting, fish-like stench and it gave off a shimmering, green light, which revealed innards cluttered with half-dissolved human bones. It rolled towards them along the passage like a slow-motion wave, liquid-light patterns playing across the roof and walls as it drew closer.

Dora had shrieked as soon as she'd seen it. She was still shrieking now, instead of turning to run. Harry didn't react much more sensibly, wrapping his arms around her in a futile attempt at protection.

'This way,' Rory cried, yanking them both backwards

They stumbled away. The hellish thing pursued, but it moved ponderously. Rory glanced back once, seeing its immense, jellified bulk filling the passage for several dozen metres.

On venturing down to the lower levels via an escalated staircase, they'd entered a warren of tunnels and culverts, all half-buried in rubble. Progress was agonisingly slow. Initially they hadn't worried too much about that, because they had no idea where they were supposed to be going anyway, but now with a predator on their trail, it was easy to panic.

'We have to get out of here,' Dora wept, as they turned corner after corner, but always found more stretches of derelict conduit ahead.

'I'll fix this,' Harry tried to reassure her, at which she thumped his chest angrily.

'How are *you* going to fix it, Harry? I bet you don't even know how you got us into this, do you? And where's Sophie? What kind of danger is our daughter in at this moment? Are you going to fix it for her?'

'This way!' Rory shouted. He'd scouted a few metres ahead, and now came running back. 'There's an old shaft leading up.'

The entrance to the shaft was littered with broken bricks, though steel cables were dangling down it, and on one side there was a set of rungs embedded into the concrete. Arm over aching arm, they ascended, their wet, ragged clothes clinging like second skins. The next level was a tiled passage with steel doors down either side. Some of these stood open on tiny cement cells.

'Looks like a prison,' Harry said.

'I think you're right,' Rory replied. 'I heard something about the Torodon using convict labour.'

Harry mopped sweat from his grimy brow. 'Could be

useful. Where there's a prison, there are weapons.'

Dora gazed at him with weary disbelief. 'What are you talking about?'

'Prisoners are always stockpiling weapons. It's a gang culture thing.'

Rory was thoughtful. 'The Doctor mentioned there was rioting here.'

'Who's the Doctor?' Harry asked.

'Just a friend.'

'For heaven's sake!' Dora interjected. 'If there are any weapons, they'll be sticks and stones. What good is that going to do?'

'It's better than nothing,' Rory said. 'There might even be a protected area where we can hold out. Come on!'

'How fascinating,' the Doctor said, gazing at the blob of vitreous material unfolding along the passage towards them. 'That's an oggle. From Gigantia's sea of dust.'

'How fascinating,' Krelbin agreed, lifting his Eradicator to his shoulder.

'I thought these imported life forms were just obstacles,' the Doctor said. 'I wasn't aware we got points for shooting them.'

'We don't.' Krelbin took aim. 'But it's in our way.'

'Hadn't thought of that.' The Doctor raised his transmat-rifle and fired first. The electric-blue beam rocketed along the dingy passage, engulfing the glutinous monstrosity in a glaring flash. A second later, the passage was clear.

Krelbin lowered his weapon, his lips taut with annoyance. The Doctor hadn't cost him points, but he'd cost him a kill, and where Colonel Krelbin was concerned that was much the same thing.

The Doctor, meanwhile, was wondering if it had been a rash act, saving the oggle's life. It was a simple, amoeboid creature, with no real awareness. He hadn't wanted to see it eradicated, but the net result was that he'd used up his second charge. He could now only fire the rifle one more time.

'Krauzzen was right,' Zubedai said from behind, he and a couple of the other hunters catching up with them. He lifted his laser-sighted visor. 'The targets have divided into two groups. The larger group is headed for the power plant.'

'In which case we should divide our forces,' the Doctor said. 'I'm going to stick with this smaller group. Good luck to the rest of you.'

Zubedai looked surprised. 'You'll blow any chance for high scoring.'

'You can keep it.' The Doctor took aim at an imaginary quarry. 'For me, it's all about the hunter and his prey. Skill and cunning, tracking and hunting, ducking and weaving. Whatever. A one-on-one contest suits me just as well.'

'I'm sure it does,' Krelbin said. 'Except that the tracks suggest there are three in this smaller group. I wouldn't want even a braggart like you to be overwhelmed.' His sweaty, scarred face gleamed with malice. 'So I'll stay with you.'

Zubedai and his party retreated into the darkness, and the Doctor and Krelbin proceeded alone. Krelbin did most of the tracking, his practised eye detecting minute clues: a footprint on the edge of a mouldy brick, a fragment of rust knocked from a jutting pipe. That made him useful, though he was also, of course, a big problem. The Doctor had no idea which party Rory was now with. He'd opted to follow the smaller group because he'd been hoping to shake off the rest of the hunters. He hadn't counted on Krelbin accompanying him.

'In case you were wondering,' Krelbin said as they scrambled up a derelict shaft. 'Zubedai and the others are no loss. I'm sure you've realised they're nothing more than bored billionaires, weekend warriors who've no idea what constitutes a fine kill.' He clambered out onto the next level, a dim passage that looked like part of a prison. 'Zubedai is the most pathetic. He actually believes that his life is stressful.'

'Actually, Colonel,' the Doctor replied, 'I'm more interested in *you*. It's surprising that a *real* soldier draws any satisfaction from facing unarmed opponents.'

Krelbin advanced, scanning the floor. 'We're between wars, Doctor, or hadn't you noticed? My regiment has been in garrison for several years, and it's mindlessly frustrating.'

'Did you know Lord Krauzzen in the military?'

'*Lord* Krauzzen?' Krelbin scoffed. 'I love the way these gangland figures adopt aristocratic titles.'

'But did you?'

'Never had dealings with him before this venture. I was in the Galactic Marine Corps. He and that maniac sidekick of his, Zarbotan, were SAB – elite commandos, constantly in action. They must be proud of the career paths they're following now.'

'If you dislike them so much, why are you cooperating with them?'

'They're a necessary evil. I need to keep in trim. But at

some point Torodon will be fighting a real enemy again, and we should wipe out these space vermin at the same time.'

'You aren't afraid they'll overhear you?'

'This is the Prison of Gorgoror, Doctor. These lower sections are vaulted with lead and reinforced concrete. There are no cameras down here, and no audio censors can penetrate.'

The Doctor wasn't sure about that, and neither, he suspected, was Colonel Krelbin, though clearly he didn't care. Krelbin had huge confidence in his own ability to wreak destruction, and probably with good reason.

They ascended another two levels, occasionally delaying to check for tracks, but eventually found themselves back among surface buildings. Much caging was in evidence: bars on windows, bars across doors. Some rooms were blackened shells.

'There was trouble here,' the Doctor said.

'There was always trouble in these off-world prisons. Criminal scum thought they had a right to an easy life. And the authorities' response, eventually, was to let them.'

'You'd have had a different solution, I imagine?'

'Show trials for the ringleaders, followed by public executions. Even harder labour for all the others. I'd teach them the price of transgressing Torodon law.'

Colonel Krelbin's inability to apply this 'moral' sense to his own behaviour might have amused the Doctor had it not frightened him. If he hadn't realised before that he was stuck here with a madman, he certainly did now.

Before he could ponder this predicament further, he saw something that brought him to a halt. They'd reached an intersection, but the left-hand passage had been marked on its facing wall with what looked, at first glance, like a smiling mouth drawn in charcoal. The Doctor recognised it as representing a crack in reality – which meant that Rory was the artist.

'Something interesting?' Krelbin asked.

'No, not really.' The Doctor pointed left. 'I suggest this way.'

'That only leads to the quarries and the work camp.'

'You can go another way, if you want.'

'No, we'll stick together. But this symbol on the wall – does it mean something?'

The Doctor shrugged. 'Prison graffiti, I imagine.'

Krelbin regarded him coolly. 'I'll stick with you, Doctor, but I hope you aren't holding out on me. I'd hate to think you're not the friend you claim to be.'

'Well, Colonel,' the Doctor winked, 'having heard your true feelings about our fellow hunters, I guess you know all there is about false friends.' He set off walking.

Krelbin followed, his mouth curved in a silent snarl.

Chapter
24

Rory and Harry were staggered by what lay in front of them.

They'd emerged from a series of gutted rooms, only to find themselves teetering on the edge of a titanic gorge criss-crossed at various levels by metal skywalks. Some of these looked to be bearing railway lines – like 'mineral lines' on Earth – though many of their supports had rotted away, and they were sagging or, in some cases, had collapsed completely. The floor of the gorge was dotted with the rusted relics of digging machinery and the shells of burned-out works buildings; the walls were pockmarked with what looked like manmade tunnel entrances.

They stood in respectful silence. Only Dora seemed unimpressed. She was pale as milk and shaking, as she leaned against a stone buttress. Harry finally noticed.

'You all right?' he asked.

She mumbled inaudibly.

'Rory… Something's wrong with Dora!'

Rory looked her over. 'Delayed shock,' he said. 'She needs rest. But not here.' He pointed to the far side of the gorge, where, perched on a parapet, there was something that looked like a medieval castle, though it had been made from plates of riveted steel. 'If that's where the inmates were billeted. We might be able to make it secure. Just till help arrives.'

'You're sure help *will* arrive?'

'I'm certain,' Rory said. He turned to the door behind them, took the lump of charcoal from his pocket and again inscribed a jagged mouth.

'What is that sign?' Harry asked. 'You've made it several times now.'

'It might just be our salvation. Let's find a way over there.'

They'd emerged onto a narrow ledge. It had a safety barrier, though in parts this had broken away, so they stayed well clear of the parapet, beyond which there was a drop of several hundred metres. They moved in single file, Dora stumbling between the two men. Every so often they came to a doorway. Glancing through, they saw the interiors of old machine houses or storage areas – bare and damp, with broken hinges hanging from walls, struts of metal jutting up where appliances had once been connected. In one, there was a line of hooks with what looked like biohazard suits hanging from them, alongside a row of upright steel containers.

'Lockers,' Harry said, entering and opening a couple, only to find them empty. 'Damn! Thought there might be something we could use.'

They went back outside – and stopped dead.

Down on the canyon floor, there was a scurrying

motion. Neither man said a word as he focused on a fast-moving, insect-like object. It had six jointed legs, which moved in a blur. Even from this distance, they could see light glinting from its shiny, red and black striped carapace.

'What on earth...?' Harry said slowly.

'Nothing on Earth,' Rory replied. 'But it must be the size of a tank.'

'It moves like one, too. Only faster.'

Whatever the insect was – and it *was* an insect, for they could now see its antennae twitching – it raced along the gorge at astonishing speed, scampering over obstacles with no difficulty.

'Is it my imagination or is it coming this way?' Harry said.

'I wish it was your imagination,' Rory said, spinning around. Maybe fifty metres ahead, the ledge projected further out via a manmade concrete lip, which was braced underneath with colossal girders. There looked to be a line of vehicles on top of it. It was possibly a terminus for one of the mineral lines.

'This way!' he shouted.

'*Rory!*'

Dora had suddenly collapsed into Harry's arms – she seemed catatonic. White-faced with fright, he peered into the gorge; the insect horror had reached the foot of the cliff wall, and was now ascending.

'If we try and carry her, we're done for,' Rory said, darting into the room where the lockers were contained and opening one. 'In here.'

'We're leaving her behind?' Harry said, incredulous.

'Concealing her. We'll distract it, try to lure it away.'

Harry might have objected further, but he knew there was no time. They manhandled the unconscious woman into the container, closed its door and rushed back outside. A quick glance over the parapet revealed that the insect was less than thirty metres below, and climbing swiftly.

They raced along the ledge to the concrete lip, which they saw was indeed a kind of siding where wheeled tubs, presumably designed to carry ore and raw minerals, were stored. One was seated at the head of a track, which dipped down across the gorge like a roller-coaster ride.

The insect had now reached the ledge, almost exactly at the point where the door gave through to the locker room. It surmounted the safety barrier, but then halted. Its head lolled from side to side, as its antennae twitched.

'It's going to find her,' Harry moaned.

Rory assessed the truck sitting on the railway track. It was a simple affair, designed to be pushed or pulled. The only thing preventing it rolling down the steep track was a brake at its rear, which was currently locked.

'Harry, get into this!'

'What?'

'Just do it!' Rory grabbed a lump of shale and bowled it, cricket-ball style, at the insect, striking it on the eye. It swung towards them, and advanced.

Rory spun back to the truck, climbing onto its rear section and kicking at the brake. Harry jumped up alongside him, scrambling into the tub, finding it half-filled with rubble and water.

The truck remained stationary.

Rory leaped down again, looking beneath the vehicle to see if something was obstructing it. There was nothing there, but the undercarriage was eaten with rust.

Behind him, a demonic chittering sound grew steadily louder.

'*Rory!*' Harry bellowed.

Rory braced himself against the truck's rugged bodywork, and gave it a massive shove. It moved slightly.

'We've got to run!' Harry said, half climbing out again.

Rory's shout was a gunshot. 'Stay there! *Heee…aaave!*'

The truck shifted forward again, with a squeal of corroded metal. The chittering sound now rang in their ears.

'*Rory, it's too late!*'

'One more!' Rory spat through gritted teeth.

He threw himself against the truck, his grimacing face a mask of sweat. The chains of rust gave, and the truck moved properly. Rory felt the ground slip from beneath his feet, but dragged himself up and charged at the vehicle again, bending his back as he slammed into it, arms outspread. The truck picked up momentum, rolling freely along the lines. Gravity started to lend a hand. Harry shouted hysterically as he fixed on what was close behind them. Rory now had to run just to keep up, but when he felt the tracks vibrate beneath him as six giant feet came pounding in pursuit, it was all the impetus he needed.

He flung himself forward, hooking his elbows over the truck's rim – just as it began to barrel downhill. Harry leaned over and, grabbing him by the belt, pulled him in. They now sped over a vast chasm, but the pursuing monster was still in touch. Rory, lying in the bilge at the bottom of the tub, looked up and saw a grotesque shape land on the back of the truck. Harry shouted madly.

This close, the insect-thing was almost too much to comprehend. A pair of bulbous, multifaceted eyes burned crimson. Mandibles large enough to masticate human bone snapped open, strands of sticky digestive fluid dangling between them. Rory was half-paralysed with fright as the thing reached a tapering, bony feeler over the rim towards him.

Then something heavy and metallic swept down and dealt it a terrific blow in the face. It was Harry. He was standing up in the truck with what looked like an old shovel. He struck it in the face again, a massive two-handed blow, but the monster clung on. Harry hit it a third time and a fourth, making savage impact on each occasion – but to no avail. It drew itself further over the rim, but now Rory joined the attack, grabbing hunks of rubble from the bottom of the tub and smashing them on its skull. Still it clambered in, its burning eyes hypnotic.

'Hack it!' Rory shouted hoarsely. 'Cut it! Like with an axe!'

Harry understood and swung the blade edge-on. Rough and blunt as it was, the first blow alone split the thing's carapace, black humours spurting out.

Suddenly the thing's grip was precarious. The second chop followed the first into the same wound, opening up a hideous breach. A flood of corruption burst out, and, with its antennae twitching madly, the monster fell back from the vehicle, tumbling along the track and vanishing into the gulf below.

The wagon jolted over some fault in the line, and Harry crashed down on top of Rory, squashing the breath from him. The truck careered downhill, working its way along the network of tracks, turning sharply as it racketed through points systems, banking around curves, steadily gaining speed. All the way, Rory and Harry lay senseless, completely oblivious to the danger.

Chapter
25

'It's kill or be killed on Gorgoror,' a gangster commented.

Two of them were watching a screen in the Salon on the *Ellipsis*. They'd been channel-hopping through a variety of images from the surface, finally settling on the labour camp. The drama unfolding there now seemed to have ended, and the mineral truck on which the two humans had narrowly evaded death was negotiating its way to the bottom of the gorge.

'Turn that off!' Xaaael said irritably. He was seated at a nearby table, playing himself at a game of Knight & Sword.

The other two exchanged knowing grins. They knew what irked him. Lord Krauzzen had taken personal charge of the Observation Booth on the surface but, instead of trusting the *Ellipsis* to his nominal second-in-command, had given it to his bodyguard and chief enforcer, Zarbotan – someone Xaaael regarded as a brute thug with no finesse. They sauntered away, leaving him brooding.

'What's the matter, Lord Xaaael?' someone else asked. 'Will no one will play you because they know what a cheat you are?'

Xaaael glared up. Amy was collecting empties from the surrounding tables.

'Hold your tongue, girl! You speak if you're spoken to on the *Ellipsis*.'

'You know, my husband only made that mistake because he fell for your goading. It's a pity you didn't pick on me. I'm not so easily intimidated.'

'Indeed?'

Amy glanced at the table in front of him. Again, it was laid with black cloth and marked with gold squares. Xaaael was moving plastic counters around it. Some lay face down, but others were face up and bore different coloured designs. It looked like a combination of backgammon and solitaire. She didn't know how to play either, but at this moment was prepared to busk it.

'We have games like this on Earth,' she said. 'And I'm regarded as an expert.'

'I'd be more impressed if you were an expert deckhand. These tables need a touch more polish. Not to mention the floor.'

'Afraid to take me on?'

Xaaael sneered. 'Your servitude here will not last for ever. You should mind your manners, lest the decision how to end it ever rests with me. Now get out of my sight.'

Knowing better than to push her luck too hard, Amy turned away.

'Besides,' he added, 'I only play competitively when there's a prize worth winning.'

She turned back. 'And if I told you I had such a prize?'

'You have nothing I couldn't take from you right now if I so wished.'

'The knowledge of how to open our spacecraft, perhaps?'

He glanced up again.

'I know you've tried to get in and failed,' she went on. 'I also know you're thinking that anything so well protected must be very valuable. And you're right. Though you've no idea how valuable.'

He almost looked amused. 'And you'll give me the opportunity to win this intelligence?'

'Just think how much credit you'd have with Lord Krauzzen.'

Xaaael's cobalt eyes gleamed. Possibly he was thinking *beyond* winning credit with Lord Krauzzen. 'And if *you* win?' he asked.

She shrugged. 'Longer rest periods. A private berth so I don't have to share with the other girls. Your guarantee that I won't be sent to Gorgoror.'

'You ask a lot.'

'Sorry.' Now it was Amy's turn to sneer. 'I mistook you for someone who often plays for high stakes.' She made to walk away.

'Wait a minute.' He indicated the black cloth. 'You know this game, you say?'

'Sure.'

Xaaael glanced around. It wouldn't do for him to be seen pitting himself against a mere slave girl. 'On the next deck down, we have cabins reserved for private entertainment. One of them belongs exclusively to me.'

'I'm aware of that.'

'Meet me there.' He stood up. 'And bring your secret knowledge. You'll soon be sharing it.'

'You're familiar with this creature?' Krelbin asked.

'Aren't you?' the Doctor said. 'I mean, having hunted on Gorgoror so often.'

'Krauzzen restocks the wildlife before each hunt. I've never seen this species before, but it wouldn't be here unless it was highly dangerous.'

The Doctor made a show of lowering his transmat-rifle. 'On this occasion, Lord Krauzzen made a mistake. This is a shologgi from the planet Pyrites. It's a herbivore, and inclined to be docile.'

They'd been making their way through the section of the prison connected to the labour camp, advancing along a concrete gantry, at the end of which a stairway led down to another barred-off security area, when they'd suddenly found this creature blocking their path. It was a great ape, covered with shaggy red hair. It was also huge; on its hind legs, it would probably tower to two and a half metres or more. Its broad, sloping shoulders implied phenomenal strength. Its arms were heavy, knotted with muscle. But at this moment, it was sitting at the foot of the staircase, its eyes half-closed.

Krelbin raised his Eradicator. 'We should dispense with it anyway.'

'And alert our real prey? Good plan,' the Doctor said. 'How much further ahead can they be? They must be exhausted by now, but if they hear gunfire they'll simply run again.'

Krelbin paused. 'What do you propose?'

'We edge past.'

'Are you serious?'

'Absolutely. You see the hatch on the other side of it?'

The shologgi was slumped to the left, which allowed a narrow passage between itself and the right-hand wall. A few metres beyond it, there was a heavy steel bulkhead through which a circular hatch connected with the next section.

'The shologgi could never fit through that tiny aperture,' the Doctor said. 'Once we're through there, we can just walk away with no danger it may follow. Here – let me show you.'

As the Doctor descended towards the beast, it watched his approach, but with an uninterested, dull-witted expression. He halted a couple of steps above it, and glanced back. 'The whole of life is one big gamble, wouldn't you say, Colonel?'

'Not for you, I don't think, Doctor. I imagine there are few occasions when you don't stack the odds in your favour.'

The Doctor continued down, treading softly when he reached the bottom and sidling past the animal. Its head turned as it tracked his progress, but still its gaze was lidded. 'Easy does it, old fella,' the Doctor said soothingly. 'I'm not your enemy.'

It made no move, except to lazily scrape a hand across its hairy belly. Once he was clear, the Doctor walked to the hatch, where he stopped and turned back.

'You see?' he shouted. 'The solution is not always to pack overwhelming ordnance. Understanding alien life forms can be just as effective.'

'Spare me the lecture.' Krelbin slung his Eradicator

over his shoulder, and commenced a wary descent.

'Of course, out in the wild, appearances can be deceptive.'

Krelbin reached the foot of the stair, and began to negotiate the narrow path leading past the shologgi. It was only a few metres in length, but once again, though the animal watched him, it appeared groggy, uninterested.

'Especially when a creature has been so abused that its true nature is lost,' the Doctor added. 'Take the shologgi. On Pyrites, they were trained for gladiatorial combat. Needless to say, the training methods had to be extraordinarily brutal, barbarising them into something that nature never intended.'

Krelbin was still edging past the beast, but now, sensing a change in tone, glanced towards the Doctor and saw that he'd produced something from under his jacket. He didn't recognise the sonic screwdriver.

'The signal for them to fight is always the same,' the Doctor said. 'A high-pitched whistle.' He briefly activated the screwdriver, which gave off a short, intense bleep.

With a savage grunt, the shologgi sat upright, the eyes under its bony, furrowed brow suddenly fixed on Krelbin with a feral gleam.

Krelbin froze. His Eradicator hung on his back, his pistol at his hip, but the brute was less than a metre away; he'd reach neither in time.

'And that was only a millisecond,' the Doctor said cheerfully. 'Imagine what would happen if I gave it a real blast. Now… this is going to be so simple that even a bone-headed militarist like you will get it, Colonel. You're going to draw your two firearms and slide them across the floor to me. Understand?'

'Doctor, I'll kill you for—'

'*Do you understand?* Because believe me, the shologgi will fully understand the signal I'll be sending it if you don't.' He brandished the sonic screwdriver. 'Beep-beep!'

Krelbin hardly dared glance at him. The shologgi leaned even closer, a low growl rumbling inside it. Drool hung in strands from its maw.

Swallowing hard, Krelbin did as he was asked – first drawing his pistol and lowering it to the floor. Then unslinging the Eradicator from his back.

'Very slowly,' the Doctor advised him. 'I only have to press this button...'

Eyes locked on the predator leaning over him, Krelbin placed the Eradicator down. With a nudge of his boot, he kicked both guns across the floor, to where the Doctor collected them.

'Good soldier,' the Doctor said, retreating towards the circular hatch. 'I'm off now. Oh, but once I'm through here I still intend to trigger this device. That means the shologgi will jump on you with everything it's got. Unless, of course you're a very fast runner.'

Krelbin now *did* glance at him, as baffled as he was angry.

'That's right,' the Doctor said, grinning as he clambered backwards through the opening. 'I'm going to give you what so many other poor wretches down here have never had – a chance. Shall we say ten seconds? One – two – three...'

Krelbin braced his back against the wall as he slid towards the foot of the stair, though the shologgi eyed him with cold hatred every inch of the way. Once he reached the first step, he galloped upward as fast as he could, sprinting off along the high gantry.

The Doctor gave him more than ten seconds – closer to forty, as he was distracted by the two new weapons he'd acquired. Eventually he located a shaft that looked like a well, and dropped them down it. Almost as an afterthought, he triggered the sonic screwdriver, which this time emitted a whistle so high-pitched that even he couldn't hear it. The shologgi responded with an ear-shattering roar, and, leaping to its feet, went charging up the stairway in pursuit of the fleeing Krelbin.

In the Observation Booth, one of Krauzzen's henchmen stood up from his chair, regarding his monitor with astonishment.

'No wonder this Doctor calls himself "the deadliest hunter",' he exclaimed. 'Looks like he's started eliminating the opposition!'

Krauzzen was at the other end of the chamber, relaxed in his command chair. He jumped up and came over. 'What's that?'

The gangster who'd spoken was called Zalizta. He it was who'd provided some of the captives after a recent trip to Earth with Zarbotan. He was small by Torodon standards and inclined to panic in a crisis. But Krauzzen held him to be loyal. Zalizta pointed with a shaking finger at the grainy screen, on which a vast, hairy shape lumbered at speed along a stone gantry, before vanishing from view.

'What happened?' Krauzzen demanded.

'The Doctor deliberately put Krelbin out of the hunt.'

The other gangsters looked at each other, amazed –

not least because the thought of anyone getting the better of a one-man army like Krelbin was quite a shock.

'Isn't that outside our rules?' someone asked.

'How can it be?' Krauzzen said, half to himself. 'We don't have any rules.

Chapter
26

'**You keep putting off** the inevitable, girl, but at some point we must play this game for real,' Xaaael snapped.

'Would you consider it fair if we played for a prize like this, and I was hindered because I didn't know the rules properly?' Amy asked indignantly.

Xaaael reorganised the counters on the black cloth. 'A couple more rounds, and then we play for real. Madam Xagra will have noted your absence by now.'

'I'm sure this isn't the first time a girl has disappeared into your quarters.'

'You're sure of a lot of things for someone who has no status here.'

'I don't need status when I have the TARDIS.'

He eyed her again. 'That's what it's called, this box – the TARDIS?'

'If you win, I'll even tell you what "TARDIS" means.'

'Just don't disappoint me. You won't like me when I'm disappointed.'

'Have another drink,' she suggested.

'I will. But don't think this will win you any favours.'

Amy had already spent enough time in Torodon male society to know they enjoyed two main alcoholic beverages. *Disdamil* was a fruit-based, low-percentage drink, which could be taken in relatively large quantities without it having a noticeable effect. But *ballomol* was a spirit, and much stronger – Torodon men only indulged in this towards the end of a working day, when they could sleep off its effects. The interesting thing about *ballomol* was that it was a clear fluid with no scent. It could be added to a jug of *disdamil*, and a drinker would not notice the difference. This was exactly what Amy had done – dosed four jugs of *disdamil* with *ballomol*, before carrying them to Xaaael's private apartment – a seedy-looking cabin filled with cushions and lurid orange light. She'd placed the jugs on his gaming table as a peace offering.

'Careful,' he'd growled. 'Don't spill anything on the black cloth. No gamer allows his cloth to be sullied.'

'I'm sorry,' she'd said, sitting at the opposite end of the table.

He had now drained two of the jugs and was starting on the third. She watched him carefully as he rather laboriously attempted to explain the rules of Knight & Sword yet again. The spiked drink was taking effect.

'Are you feeling all right?' she asked tentatively.

'Of course. We have to get on with this game if I'm to acquire your TARDIS before Krauzzen returns.' His gaze was foggy as he regarded her. 'You understand now?'

'I think so. Oh, but I'm not sure about the Royal.' She pointed to a pink counter.

'You stupid young fool!' he slurred. 'That isn't the

Royal, that's the Imp. These are the Royals.' He indicated a pair of blue and green counters. 'Now… these can only be played when… when…' Xaaael's eyes were suddenly rolling. He lifted the fourth jug and quaffed its contents in two great gulps, after which he smacked his lips. 'That's… better. Needed to clear my… my…'

He fell sideways from the table.

Amy crouched alongside him, where he now lay snoring. He was wearing his usual kimono, but she'd been watching her captors carefully. Inside it, where a breast pocket would normally be, she found a pouch containing a plastic wallet. When she opened this, it was packed with slide-cards. She counted thirty in total. None of their insignia mean anything to her, but if necessary she would try them all. She pocketed them and moved to the cabin door, opening it slightly and peering into a deserted companionway.

'Harry!' Rory shouted, brushing the dust and ash from Harry's lifeless face.

'Go away,' Harry groaned. 'I'm unconscious.'

Rory laughed with relief.

'What happened?' Harry asked.

'We made it.'

Harry sat up painfully, and glanced around. Alongside them, the mineral truck was half-buried in a great mound of cinders. About five metres overhead, the mineral line simply ended; the twisted, rusty stumps of its rails jutted into empty air. Glancing further afield, he saw that they were at the bottom of the gorge; on all sides lay the burnt skeletons of earth movers, the empty shells of buildings.

'And where have we made it to?' he said. 'Hell's car

park?'

'At least we're alive.' Rory helped him to his feet.

Memories now rushed back to Harry. He focused on the cutting high in the opposite cliff face. 'Dora's still up there…'

'She'll be safer where she is than with us.'

'Yeah, but for how long?'

Rory put a hand on his shoulder. 'We'll go back for her. But first why don't we check out the barrack block, while we're here?'

Harry glanced behind them. A footway snaked its way up a rugged slope, at the top of which towered the riveted steel fortress.

They trudged towards it, dusting themselves down.

'You saved our bacon back there,' Rory said.

'First thing I've got right since we arrived,' Harry muttered.

'How'd you and your family end up in this mess? You obviously weren't nabbed for being economic migrants.'

Harry recounted the events that had led to his family's capture, paying particular attention to his own bungling efforts. When he'd finished they walked on in silence. They were now tramping uphill, dirt adhering to their sweat.

'Why'd you leave the police, anyway?' Rory asked. 'Early retirement?'

'Hah, I wish.' Harry said nothing else for a few moments, but then admitted: 'I was fed up with uniform duties. Walking a beat, driving a panda car. I'd passed my sergeant's exam, but there was no sign of promotion. I'd applied to CID dozens of times. They didn't want to know. I was good at my job, but I wasn't an academic. A "woodentop", was the phrase. And I got bored with it. Felt I'd accomplished nothing, was going nowhere – all that stuff you imagine has been invented just to torture you when you've got a job, and miss so much when you haven't. Anyway, I'd just started a week of nights and I really wasn't up for it. I parked a few times and had a kip. Got caught by the inspector and rollocked. Later in the week, a motorist stopped me and asked for directions to a road called Ravenbrook Avenue, and I told him. What I didn't realise, because my head wasn't in the game, was that this fella was about three times over the drink-drive limit. Not only that, he was on his way to assault his sister's ex. He crashed his car en route, caused a load of damage and still went and committed the crime. When he finally got nicked, it came out that I'd spoken to him beforehand and let him go. That was seen as a major abrogation of duty. One black mark too many.'

They'd now reached the top of the slope and the main barrack building. The mud in front of it was criss-crossed by caterpillar tracks. The remnant of a heavy steel gate lay to one side. It was covered in burns and dents, as if small arms had been discharged at it. At first, Rory was too distracted by all this to speak.

'No comment?' Harry asked.

'What… oh, don't beat yourself up. It's not like any of us are perfect. I'm only here because I made one hell of a mistake too.'

Harry looked surprised. '*You* did? I had you tagged as some kind of space ranger.'

'You ever heard of a space ranger called Rory?'

They ventured through the gate, passing beneath an arch and along an entry tunnel, the end of which had been blocked by a barricade assembled from beams, planks and sheets of metal welded clumsily together. A central portion of this had been driven back, and again the ground was deeply rutted. Rory sidled his way past, at which point he halted.

'You brought us here to find something to fight back with, didn't you?' he said.

'It was a chance,' Harry replied, following. 'Probably not much of one.'

'You reckon?'

Beyond the barricade lay a courtyard littered with all kinds of improvised weapons: bats, cleavers, spears, shields. They were old and rusty of course, but many still looked serviceable.

'We may be pair of losers, Harry,' Rory said. 'But at least we're starting to even the odds.'

Chapter
27

Amy headed to the Engineering section without interference, which was one advantage a slave caste had here. As long as they looked like they were working, they tended to be flyspecks beneath everyone else's notice. She'd equipped herself with cleaning materials, and hurried down to the lower decks, stopping here and there to polish balustrades or sweep stretches of already immaculate carpet.

In Engineering itself, the occasional crewman sauntered by, but again she pretended to be working and they ignored her. When she reached the door to the Secure Hold, there was nobody around. She filched the pile of entry cards from under her tunic, hugging the door in an effort to keep them hidden. The infrastructure on this level was bare and utilitarian: not just catwalks and caged machinery, but lagged piping, vaulted archways formed from unpainted steel. No camera that she could see was filming her, but she didn't know that for sure. One card after another went through the slide-lock, to no effect. It occurred to her that these failed attempts might be activating alarms elsewhere – maybe on the Bridge – but it was too late to worry about that now. Speed was suddenly everything.

'Amy Pond!' a voice shrilled behind her.

Amy twirled around.

Madam Xagra's travelling-eye was hovering there. Its cat-green viewing portal, which was about the size of a normal eye, seemed to blink as it regarded her.

'Report to Housekeeping at once, where you will explain your behaviour!'

'Can't I explain now… ma'am?' Amy said, shoving the entry-cards behind her back.

'What exactly are you doing?'

Amy shrugged awkwardly. 'You see, well… when I was cleaning down here earlier, I thought the door to the Secure Hold could do with a bit of spit and polish. So when the opportunity arose, I just, well, I sort of…'

The travelling-eye blinked again, as if waiting for a part of the excuse it could actually believe.

'I'm only being diligent, ma'am,' Amy said.

'You are an insolent girl and will be punished regardless of this explanation! No menial may deviate from their daily patterns of duty unless at my express command. Return to Housekeeping at once!'

'You know, ma'am, I don't think I'll bother.'

There was a long silence, and then: 'Well, miss, I suspected this on our first day together. The instant I saw you, I thought, "Here is a wilful girl. She must broken; she must be tamed. This is one who will learn the value of humility—"'

Amy interrupted: 'Sorry, ma'am, but I've only got

one more thing to say to you. And that is…' She swung her dustpan. There was a deafening clang as impact was made. *'She shoots, she scores!'*

Amy watched, delighted, as the travelling-eye rocketed away into the far distance. That was when she heard gruff male voices and heavy feet approaching.

'Oh heck!' She spun back to the door and tried more entry-cards.

She'd gone through eight, and voices were echoing around her, when there came a bleeping from the mechanism, and the door slid open. She scurried through and it slammed behind her just as quickly.

The Secure Hold was not what she'd anticipated. She'd half-expected to find the place heaped with glittering treasure, like some futuristic dragon's cave. Instead, she was at the top of a ramp, which rolled down into a warehouse-type environment arrayed with tall steel racks on which crates and boxes of every description were stacked. The place was dim – lit only by low-key, greenish light.

Amy sat down and took the TARDIS key from her left boot. She hurried to the bottom of the ramp and along several aisles – before hearing a muffled thumping from somewhere close by. Along one bulkhead, there was a row of slide-doors, all closed. The noise was coming from the second one along. Someone was on the other side of it, shouting and pounding.

On the basis that her enemy's enemy was likely to be her friend, and therefore someone who might help – she tried more entry-cards. The tenth was accepted. The door hissed open, revealing a tiny, egg-shaped room.

A Torodon male all but fell out of it.

'Thank… thank you,' he gasped. 'Thought… I was going to die in there…'

His white hair, unusually short for a Torodon, had been dyed blond, and now hung in a stringy, sweaty mop. The silvery pallor of his face was smeared with what looked like flesh-toned make-up. Stranger still were his clothes; they consisted of socks, a pair of undershorts and a rather grubby bathrobe.

'Who are you?' Amy asked, baffled.

'They… they had no choice. They had to keep me locked up.'

'Who are you?'

'The name's Kalik Xorax. You may know me by another name – Pangborne. Grant Pangborne.'

When Dora came round, she found herself in an upright metal box, which smelled of oil and dust, and admitted no light. Immediately she panicked, throwing her body from side to side, crying aloud.

This hullaballoo lasted several seconds before she heard the *clunk* of a turning handle, and the lid – or door, as it transpired – was opened. She staggered forward, grabbing what felt like the lapels of a tweed jacket, before sinking to her knees, panting.

'Hello?' the Doctor said. 'You're making an awful lot of noise.'

Dora gawked up at him. 'Oh… I… Who are you?'

'I'm the Doctor.' He gently disentangled himself from the clutching hands.

'You're a doctor?' At first she tittered, but then began to laugh hysterically. 'Are you sure… are you sure you're not an architect'?'

'Architect? Why would I be an architect. "The Architect" – no, doesn't have the same ring to it, somehow.'

Dora nodded to a section of concrete wall, where, with a chunk of charcoal, he'd been in the process of sketching out what looked like the detailed anatomy of a massive industrial complex.

'Oh, that.' The Doctor tossed the charcoal and stuck his hands into his trouser pockets. 'Just recollecting what I can about the floor-plan on this moon. Not a bad effort, if I say so myself.'

'Moon?' Dora stopped laughing and rose to her feet. 'We're on the Moon?'

'Not your moon, of course.'

She looked at him askance, wondering if any of this could be real. He said he was a doctor. And he certainly looked like one, with his dickie-bow, patched tweed jacket and ridiculous, unmanageable hair. But a doctor? Here? And where was *here*?

'Who are you?' she asked again, querulously. 'I mean, *really*?'

'I've already told you. Now, this is very interesting.' He pointed to a crudely drawn box in the sketch's top right-hand corner. 'At the north end of this industrial site, there's an abandoned rocket base, complete with its own control tower. Who are *you*, by the way?'

'Erm…' Initially Dora wasn't quite sure. 'Dora… Dora Mossop.'

He turned back to the floor-plan. 'What do you know about electromagnetic radiation, Dora Mossop?'

'Come again?'

'Wavelengths in the electromagnetic spectrum. In other words, radio.'

'Radio?'

'Yes, radio.' He glanced sidelong at her. 'I'm going to save your life. And the lives of your friends. But you'll need to do exactly as you're told, understand?'

She nodded dumbly.

'Now, if we can get to the top of that control tower, it's highly possible there'll still be a functioning radio link. It'll have been deactivated, obviously, but if *I* can't reactivate it, nobody can. Why were you in that cupboard, by the way?'

'I think I was hiding.'

'Really. What from?'

'I don't know.' Dora looked shamefaced. 'I was in a faint.'

'So somebody put you in there?'

'Harry and Rory.'

'I see. And this thing you were hiding from – did Harry and Rory get away?'

'I don't know.'

'And what was it?'

'I don't know that either.'

'You don't know much, do you, Dora Mossop?'

Again her cheeks reddened. Memories of recent events were flooding back to her, but the most painful one was her attitude to Harry in the last couple of days. She'd been horribly selfish, she realised; so determined to punish him for his failures that she'd deliberately turned a blind eye to his attempts to put things right.

'Well, if you're going to come with me, that won't do,' the Doctor said. 'I need someone I can rely on.'

He seemed very young to be speaking with such authority, and yet there was an aura of calm control about him that Dora felt she could trust.

'Just tell me what you want me to do,' she said.

'Well, to start with, you can take your clothes off.'

'*What?*'

He indicated her laddered tights, knee-length skirt and muddied cardigan. 'They're not very practical. Those, however, would be.' He pointed at the row of anti-toxin suits in the corner.

'You want me to get changed?'

'Ah, good point. Don't worry, I'll wait outside.'

Before she could respond, the Doctor had left the locker room, moving out onto the ledge. His mind was already working through the possibles and probables. If Rory and this Harry person had hidden Dora, that was almost certainly because they'd concluded they had a chance to outrun their foe without the burden of a casualty – which was encouraging. He glanced down into the gorge and across to its far side. Nothing moved, which was also a positive sign. On Gorgoror, no news was good news. He switched his thoughts to the rocket base and its potential for offering them a way out. Of course, it would all depend on Amy regaining possession and control of the TARDIS, and his being able to contact her so that he could assist her in piloting it down here. First he had to find his way to the base in the quickest time possible. If he remembered rightly, he needed to veer away from the prison, and pass through the atomic power plant. They still had to locate Rory, but retrieving the TARDIS had become the imperative.

Dora reappeared, dressed as he'd instructed, in one of the anti-toxin outfits. It was actually rather fetching. Tight-fitting, and made of shiny black vinyl, it accentuated her female form, and suited her long dark hair and pretty face.

'Much better,' the Doctor said.

She shrugged. 'Don't I look a bit silly? I feel like one of those TV action girls.'

'A snivelling housewife is no good to me,' he said. 'But an action girl I can use.'

'Curiosity,' Krauzzen said. He was still inside the Observation Booth. The screen in front of him depicted the dim shapes of the Doctor and Dora making their way together along a narrow shelf of rock. 'Curiosity has always been a weakness of mine. The moment the Doctor threatened us with black-light, I ought to have known we weren't dealing with some ordinary adventurer. I should have killed him on the spot.'

'Shall I inform the *Ellipsis*?' Zalizta asked.

'Not yet. If that craft of his really is rigged to blow, it will panic them to know he's an enemy. They might try something stupid, like attempting to detach it.'

'But if that's a deception too... ?'

'We can deal with that later. Everyone, get your weapons!'

Chapter
28

Xaaael woke up on his cabin floor, after being doused with a pail of ice-cold water.

'What the devil…!' he spluttered, staggering to his feet.

'Spare me your synthetic rage, Xaaael,' Zarbotan said, hurling the pail aside. 'What duty are you supposed to be on?'

'None… since our lord and master saw fit to put command of this ship in the hands of a hulking, two-faced ape like you!'

Zarbotan leaned forward dangerously. 'Xaaael, if you have no duties at present, I will happily give you a very important one – make sure nothing else goes wrong. *Nothing!* You understand? Or you'll be held personally responsible.' And he stormed out into the companionway.

Xaaael followed him. 'What's going on?'

'It's the Earth girl, you drink-addled buffoon!'

Xaaael's fogged memory was now clearing. He felt at his breast-pouch, which was empty. 'Damn, I've been robbed! Zarbotan, that little minx has... I'll kill her!'

He dashed past Zarbotan, only to be grabbed and hurled against the bulkhead.

'You've done enough damage, Xaaael,' Zarbotan snarled. 'Get yourself in a fit state for duty and report to the Bridge.'

'But where the devil is she?'

'Where do you think? In the Secure Hold, which she's gained entry to with *your* access-card!'

Xaaael was visibly shaken. 'Well... she can't do any harm, surely? There's nothing of use to her in there.'

'Except the property you confiscated on LP9. Do you even know what that is?'

Xaaael remained blank-faced.

'Exactly,' Zarbotan said. 'For all we're aware, it could be another black-light explosive, and it's now deep in the belly of this ship.'

'I'll come with you!'

But Zarbotan threw him against the bulkhead again. 'Do as you're told, Xaaael! Go to the Bridge and take charge there!'

'But you're going down there *alone*!'

'And who else do I need?'

Xaaael didn't argue further. Resourceful as the Earth girl was, Zarbotan was the most dangerous living creature he knew – if you could honestly describe that semi-necrotic, semi-mechanical abomination as 'living'. He'd killed more men during his life than the leprous atmosphere in the mines of Gorgoror had in a hundred years.

'Zarbotan!' Xaaael shouted as the giant figure clumped away.

Zarbotan glanced back.

'Does Krauzzen know about my… indiscretion?'

'No. And pray to your gods we can keep it that way.'

In the Observation Booth, Krauzzen and his soldiers were ready to go out onto the surface.

Krauzzen had donned a special harness, in the back section of which his hover-plate was inserted. This was a small, lightweight assault craft, a simple oval-shaped board, moulded from a silver-titanium alloy and designed to carry a single infantryman to attack targets in open space. Developing full telekinetic control over these swift but silent devices was a prerequisite to enlisting in the Special Assault commandos, which was why so few Torodon, including experienced combat soldiers from other units, were ever deemed eligible.

Krauzzen slung his photon-rifle alongside his hover-plate, and holstered a pistol at his hip. His men, though unequipped with hover-plates – with the exception of Zarbotan, his outfit had never been anything but grunts – were also heavily armed.

'We've been infiltrated,' he said. 'But is this a privateer who fancies his luck, or something more sinister? I'm not sure. But we're not taking the chance. We never take chances like this. The entire operation has been compromised, and we've no choice but to respond with *extreme* action.'

They knew exactly what he meant.

Chapter
29

'**The important thing,**' **the** Doctor said, 'is that, though your husband's made mistakes, he's not the one who abducted you. He's as much a victim as you are.'

'I know,' Dora said. 'I've been hard on Harry. It's almost like I've been too obsessed with my own problems.'

'Well, any problems you may have had before will have paled into insignificance by the time we get out of this. Assuming we *do* get out of it.'

This stranger who called himself the Doctor, and who for some reason Dora had felt it safe to open up to as they'd walked and climbed and struggled through the wreckage and rubble cramming the endless underground caverns of this netherworld, had a disconcertingly frank way of speaking.

'You think we might not make it?' she asked.

'I think the odds are against us.' He stood up from the overturned bucket on which he'd been resting. 'But that doesn't mean we sit down and cry, does it?'

'No,' she agreed.

'Good.' He lowered his voice. 'You'll need to remember that, because we're being hunted. And I don't just mean by Lord Krauzzen's weekend warriors. I mean by something significantly more proficient.'

Dora stiffened where she sat. 'Another of these creatures they've put down here?'

'Don't look round! It's about sixty metres behind us, and it's been following for the last five minutes.'

'Oh my God…'

'Relax, Dora. Remember what we've just said.'

'What is it?'

'I'm not sure yet.'

The Doctor surveyed the tunnel. As far as he could tell, this was one of the connecting lines between the prison complex and the power station. It had a flat, concrete floor and a tiled arched ceiling. Parts of it had caved in and all sorts of other junk had been thrown down here, so they'd already had to negotiate heaps of shifting, razor-edged detritus. He threw another furtive glance behind them. The pursuing figure had dropped to a crouch, and was little more than a shadowy blob. From what he'd glimpsed, it was humanoid and bipedal, but covered with excessive leathery skin, which, when it moved, trailed behind it like a heavy cloak.

'Come on.' He took Dora by the arm and hauled her to her feet.

She now walked stiffly, sensing the nameless presence close behind. 'Why don't you just shoot it?' she whispered.

'I can't, and it's as simple as that.'

The Doctor didn't want to send another alien monster

back to the police holding cells on LP9 – it was anyone's guess how much trouble the last one had caused. More importantly, he was increasingly thinking that the only way out of this mess for Dora might be to use his last transmat charge on her – to save *her* life if no one else's.

They passed under a heavy gate, before clambering upward through a mass of fallen, broken machinery festooned with loose cables. At the top of this was an entrance to a vast, complex structure, something like a three-dimensional maze of steel-mesh passages. The Doctor hesitated.

'What's the matter?' Dora asked, sweat dripping from her face.

He didn't bother explaining that from here on the way forward would be little more than a 'single file' crawlspace, and that he didn't want to be at the rear because he felt she would be too slow at the front, and yet didn't want to put Dora at the rear because he suspected that whatever was following them would have marked her as the weaker prey and might then attack. A clanking from below, as something climbed in pursuit, decided it for them.

'Go ahead,' the Doctor said.

She climbed up the narrow mesh chute first.

'Hurry!' he shouted, scrambling after her. Initially it was a vertical shaft, but soon they found themselves on the horizontal. 'More speed!' the Doctor urged.

Dora crawled along as best she could, but the grilled floor and riveted joints between its sections were hard on her hands and knees.

'Which way?' she panted when they reached a junction.

'It doesn't matter,' he replied, trying to keep the panic from his voice.

Dora opted for the right-hand path. At the next junction she took the left one, and at the one after that she went right again. There was no rhyme or reason to it, but she could sense the Doctor's urgency and her own fear was rising.

'Go up!' the Doctor now shouted. 'Take the next upward shaft. We have to get to the surface.'

She did as he said, and this was slightly easier. Climbing the steel mesh wasn't as uncomfortable as sliding across it on all fours. But by the time she reached the top, Dora was exhausted. Only adrenalin-charged desperation allowed her to manhandle a circular steel slab out of her way and climb through the hatch above. The Doctor followed, and found himself in a low-roofed cement chamber with a slot aperture, which, though it was at eye-level for them, gave out at ground level on the moon's surface. It was a blast shelter, the Doctor realised. They were inside the dome containing the power plant. He grabbed Dora's hand, and they tottered up some steps to the surface.

'Open ground,' the Doctor said. 'Now we *really* run for it.'

Dora nodded wearily, and they stumbled forward. Ahead of them, across the black plain, there towered another immense, ghostly structure: a row of colossal cones, like industrial cooling towers. Again, it was far from simple reaching them. The ground was burned and barren, and crumbled beneath their feet. The litter of refuse – everything from demolition rubble, to fallen pylons, to the smoke-blackened relics of diggers, lifters and other corroded mechanical leviathans – sent them scurrying in every direction as they tried to make progress.

Halfway across, the Doctor glanced over his shoulder. Their stalker, which had given up attempting to conceal its presence, was closing the gap between them with a series of prodigious leaps, aided by a black, leathery, parachute-like canopy. Recognising what it was, he now drove Dora mercilessly. Even when they entered the main power plant buildings, and ran down a broad concourse, he urged her on, telling her not to look back.

'What… what is that thing?' she stammered.

'An Air-Walker.'

'Air-Walker?'

'It walks on air. Well, sort of. But never mind that now!'

The next thing, they were descending to the plant's sublevels, taking a spiral stair which dropped between more layers of corroded apparatus, and running along a catwalk hemmed in by rows of vertical plastic tubes down which a glowing, yellowish glop was streaked.

'Where are we going?' Dora wailed.

The Doctor was about to reply, but just ahead one of the tubes had collapsed across the catwalk and broken. Whatever the substance in the tube was, it had melted the metal, leaving a gap of maybe two and a half metres.

'OK,' the Doctor said. 'OK, we have to jump.'

'Jump?' Dora looked at him, incredulous.

'Whatever you do, don't touch that yellow muck – it'll turn your flesh to slurry.'

Dora shook her head as she backed away. 'I can't jump that far. We'll go back.'

The Doctor took her wrist with a hand like a talon. 'Dora, we *can't* go back! The Air-Walker is already focused on sucking the marrow from our bones.'

Dora glanced over her shoulder. The catwalk led into pitch darkness. She hated herself for the weakness she was again showing, but she was so tired, and so terrified. Her next words were distraught, thickened by tears. 'There's no end to the horror in this place – it's like Hell, and there are devils round every corner.'

'What happened to the action girl I was promised?'

'That's not me.'

'Sure it is. Look… let's hold hands. So if you go, I go too. OK?'

Before she could argue, they ran forward. Dora screeched as they leapt out over what looked like a bottomless chasm. Rather to her surprise, they landed cleanly and continued running. There was an aperture ahead; they had the impression of open space, but when they scrambled through it, they found themselves on the brink of another terrifying drop.

They'd emerged into a huge chamber, which seemed to have collapsed in on itself. It was impossible to see where the roof should be. All manner of crushed, tangled wreckage had deluged down into it from overhead, and had become lodged at various levels, though the chamber's floor was actually a vast, crater-like hole, maybe eighty metres in diameter, which seemed to plummet into infinite blackness. Further avalanches, mainly consisting of concrete and shattered masonry, had spilled down the sides of it, but looked perilously steep and unstable. Other items – mainly sections from the floors above, wooden beams, warped panelling and so on – lay across one side of the hole, forming a flimsy bridge.

The Doctor started across this before Dora even had a

chance to protest.

She followed, arms outstretched for balance, trying not to think how narrow and creaky the makeshift causeway was beneath her feet. Halfway across, there were stinging pains in both earlobes as her studs were snatched out.

She yelped in pain. The Doctor, who had reached a central point, glanced back. He was in the process of adjusting the transmat-rifle at his shoulder, only to see it catapult out of his hands and go twirling downward for several metres, until its strap caught on a twisted fragment of metal jutting from the crater's side. It hung there, but turned and rotated, as if actively seeking a way to descend.

'Ahhh,' he said. 'I wondered why that thing was tugging my shoulder off.'

Dora had now reached him. She clung to him hard, unwilling to look down.

'My earrings,' she sniffled.

'Yes. We're under the point where the reactor was once located. Its magnetic core must have come loose from its housing, probably during the seismic disturbances. No wonder they evacuated this place. Anyway, in the time since it's burrowed its way down towards Gorgoror's gravitational heart. This crater must be thousands of metres deep by now. You've nothing metallic on you of any value?'

She shook her head.

'Well, I have.' He could feel his sonic screwdriver trying to dig its way through the material of his jacket pocket, as if this too was suddenly many times heavier than before. 'Time to go.'

'What about your rifle?'

The Doctor stared at her. 'Good point, yes. Valuable prototype. I'll climb down there and get it back, shall I?'

Dora shook her head again.

'Thought not.'

They stumbled across the remaining section of bridge, and reached the far side – a jagged concrete podium, jutting out over the gulf. The only way to move beyond this was via a closed steel door.

'Can't be too far to go now,' the Doctor said.

'Doctor – *look!*'

Dora was gazing back across the crater. Their pursuer had emerged into full view on the other side, and was regarding them with a smooth, featureless face. It was humanoid in outline, but taller than either of them by at least thirty centimetres, and jet black all over. Its flesh had a shiny, oily texture and was hung with a fin-like canopy.

The Doctor gave it only a sparing glance, before turning back to the steel door – to find that it wouldn't budge when he pushed against it. Dora joined him, shoving with all her might. There was no response.

'Buckled in its frame,' the Doctor said. 'Probably due to the magnetic forces in the crater.'

'OK, I'm the action girl,' Dora said, snatching up a lump of stone. 'We attack that thing as it tries to cross… *oh my word!*'

The oil-black monstrosity was now six metres up a sheer concrete pillar, climbing with the flats of its hands and feet as if they bore sucker pads.

'It's trying to find a perch,' the Doctor said. 'From which it can leap.'

'Leap?'

'Walk on air, remember? It's not called an Air-Walker for nothing. Two or three big jumps and it'll be over here with us.'

The creature was soon twelve metres up. Not far over its head, various ganglia of shredded cables and entwined fragments of hanging rubble offered the aforementioned perch.

'What do we do?' Dora said, panic rising in her voice.

'That outfit you're wearing. Are there any tools in its pockets?'

'Tools?'

'It's protective gear, Dora, for hazardous work. There may be something.'

She slapped down her sides and thighs, finding a single pouch containing a sausage-shaped packet filled with a squidgy white material.

The Doctor grinned and snatched it from her. 'Dora Mossop, you're a genius.'

'For finding wall filler? We going to be doing some DIY, Doctor? Fix the place up?'

'No, just the opposite. This is plastic explosive. Used in quarrying.'

'Oh...'

On top of everything else, while she'd been running, jumping, climbing and generally bouncing around, Dora now realised that she'd been carrying something with the potential to blow her to smithereens. In normal circumstances she might have been sick, but it was amazing how quickly you got used to intense, high-end terror.

'Stand back,' the Doctor said.

'Stand back where?'

'Just stand back.' He'd squeezed out some of the material and was now thumbing it into place around the edges of the buckled door.

'There's nowhere we can stand back.'

'Get as far as you can, and crouch low.'

Dora did as instructed, but glanced up again. The Air-Walker was at least twenty metres up the opposite wall, and crouching on the end of a broken ventilation valve. It had coiled up like a spring.

'Doctor!' she cried.

'Lie flat!' he shouted, retreating and drawing his sonic screwdriver from his pocket, though it was such an effort to hold it steady that he had to use both hands. It bucked and twisted as if eager to flit out of his grasp.

Dora could sense their dark stalker making its first leap, the membranes of skin extending between its limbs as it launched itself through the air. The Doctor looked up, and saw the creature alight on another piece of dangling wreckage. Immediately, it re-coiled itself. Two more such leaps and it would be upon them. He turned back to the door, wrestling with his screwdriver as he lay down and hit the button.

There was an ear-piercing squeal, and a thunderous *BOOM* as the blast almost swept them from the podium. When they opened their eyes, there was a dusty, smoke-filled hole where the door had stood. The Doctor jumped up, hauling Dora by her collar. They followed a passage cluttered with smouldering brick rubble. Ahead of them stood another door – but this one was open, and there was a big space beyond it.

'We're through,' the Doctor shouted.

He dragged Dora out into another vast, hangar-type

building. Its nearest exit was maybe fifty metres away, but they'd only made twenty when there was an ululating shriek overhead. As they looked up, the Air-Walker exploded out through a high vent. It briefly caught hold of another loose perch – a sagging section of roof, huge concrete cakes strung limply together by rusting wires, which now groaned alarmingly – and then sprang again, this time right at them.

The Doctor looked wildly around – there was nowhere to run, nowhere to hide.

Dora didn't even have time to scream. The horror descended like a dark angel, its membranes spread and billowing, its previously featureless head gaping to reveal row after row of knife-blade teeth.

The Doctor wrapped his arms around Dora, forcing her to the ground to shield her with his own body. But then there was a searing flash, a massive *CRACKLE* of energy – and when the Air-Walker landed beside them, it was a corpse: smoking and contorted, and giving off a foul stench of burning.

The Doctor and Dora rose back to their feet, bewildered.

'Air-Walkers live on the planet Cha-Bala,' the Doctor said sadly. 'The natives of the neighbouring Ka-Bala worship them as gods of music.'

'Gods of music?' Dora replied, barely understanding what he was saying.

He walked slowly around the charred carcass.

'They would abandon sacrificial victims on the surface of Cha-Bala, where Air-Walkers would eat them. They'd do a really thorough job, leaving nothing but hollow bones, which the Ka-Balans would recover and make into wind instruments. Apparently the sound is quite beautiful.'

Dora stared at him, perplexed.

'Ironic, eh?' He looked across the hangar, to where a tall but familiar figure in tiger-striped hunting fatigues was approaching. 'That one god of music should be brought down by another.'

Chapter
30

Kalik Xorax had tried to explain who he was and why he was being held captive, but he interspersed this so regularly with asthmatic gasps, and it was so long-winded anyway as he was clearly in a state of shock, that Amy soon got bored and recommenced her search for the TARDIS.

Xorax followed her around, still panting and jabbering. She noted a few things he said – about having betrayed Krauzzen's trust, and about how his fate would be ghastly though no one would ever know about it because he was a Torodon – but most of the rest seemed like self-justifying gibberish.

'A man has to make a living, doesn't he?' he said, as she prowled the stacks of cargo. 'I never set out intending to buy and sell people. I was an ordinary businessman. When I was exiled to Earth for malpractice, I had to put food on the table somehow. So when Lord Krauzzen contacted me, it was an offer I couldn't refuse. I mean, what are humans to me? I suppose that sounds terrible.

But I'm Torodon, a different species from you. And when you're a different species, well… it's hard to have empathy, if you know what I mean. But I'm endlessly grateful for what you've done. I can't—'

'All right!' Amy snapped. 'If you want to thank me, look for the TARDIS.'

'The TARDIS?'

'It's a tall blue box.'

'You mean like that?'

Amy glanced up to where he was pointing, and saw the TARDIS perched on a shelf about five and a half metres overhead, sandwiched between two piles of bulging plastic sacks.

'Oh,' she said. 'Erm… right. Can you help me get up there?'

'I don't think I could get myself up there.' He adopted an expression of pained frailty. 'I haven't slept or eaten for days.'

She was about to point out that his 'endless gratitude' wasn't up to very much, when she heard the slide-hiss of the entry door. Xorax glanced at her, his hollow eyes suddenly wide with fear. She motioned him to keep quiet.

From where they were, the door was out of sight, but they listened intently. It hissed closed again. She pricked her ears for the slightest sound – a whisper of voices, the creak of a boot on the polished metal floor.

But none of that came.

'We must hide,' Xorax breathed into her ear.

'I don't think anyone's come in,' she replied quietly.

'Someone has. And he'll be searching for us right now.'

'In that case I have to get up to the TARDIS.'

Xorax glanced to the top shelf again, only to shake his head and back away from her. Flattening himself on the floor, he slid his body beneath a pallet on which various machine parts glittered. Amy again listened out, but still heard no sound of approach. Xorax was peeking up at her from his place of concealment. She stuck her tongue out at him, before attempting to clamber up the great stack of shelving on her own. She was perhaps halfway up when she glanced over her shoulder, and, having a clear, unobstructed view through several other racks of goods, saw something that made her blood run cold.

It was the giant, Zarbotan.

He was now searching for her, but, to her astonishment, not by plodding around on foot – by apparently floating through mid air. She was so unable to believe the evidence of her own eyes that she remained in full view for several, near-disastrous seconds. When she suddenly realised how exposed she was, she clambered onto one of the midway shelves, and lay down. She had restricted vision from there, but could still see him. He was standing upright on some kind of silver hover-board, which could apparently move in any direction he wished. He was two aisles away, elevated to three metres in the air, and pivoting cautiously around as he scanned every level of shelving. His movements were graceful, but also rather ghostly – an effect enhanced by the dim greenish light of the hold.

Amy lay frozen as he swished past her at a lower level and disappeared round a corner. Briefly he was gone, though evidently he would soon make another pass, probably checking out the higher ledges. She glanced ruefully up at the TARDIS: so close and yet so far. With no other choice, she hung by her fingertips before dropping into the aisle and scampering away, looking for somewhere – anywhere – to hide properly.

'Well, Doctor,' Zubedai said, approaching with pulse-rifle levelled. 'It seems you've changed sides. I'm not sure that's completely a surprise.'

'What is a surprise is that *you're* the one who's caught me,' the Doctor replied.

'Ahhh!' Zubedai lifted his laser-sighted visor. 'You think a soft-living celebrity like me shouldn't have the instinct for this sort of thing?'

'I've no doubt you've got the instinct. But the ability is something else.'

'Well…' Zubedai chuckled. The parts of his face that hadn't been covered by his oxygen mask and visor were smudged with dust, suggesting that his hunt, so far, had been a lively one. 'Maybe in overhearing your explosion, I got lucky. But we all need a bit of luck.' He raised his rifle to his shoulder. 'I don't know what points I'll get for you, if any… but that's no matter. I'm content to take a share of your money.'

But before Zubedai could fire, he gave a strangled gasp of pain. The blackened carcass of the Air-Walker lay alongside him, though apparently there was still a spark of life in it; without warning, it had turned its head, and clamped its serrated teeth onto his left ankle. Zubedai's gasp became a shriek as it applied crushing pressure. Desperately, he began kicking out, raining down blows with the butt of his rifle.

It was all the distraction Dora needed.

'Doctor!' she cried, throwing something. '*The wall filler!*'

The packet of plastic explosive was still half full. By the time it landed at Zubedai's feet, the Doctor had already drawn his screwdriver and activated it.

This second explosion was much bigger than the first, throwing both fugitives to the ground, pummelling their ears. After the echoes died away, it took almost a minute for the dense cloud of smoke to clear. Cautiously, the Doctor wafted his way through. When he reached the edges of the small crater and saw the ragged remnants strewn across and around it, he could only shake his head.

'I make that Hunting Party – nil. Inconsequential Species – two.'

There was a sudden *CRACKLE* of electronic gunfire – it sounded as if it was just outside the hangar. The Doctor hurried towards the exit.

Dora stumbled after him and, when she caught up with him, peered down onto another flat wasteland dotted with ruins and the wrecks of abandoned vehicles.

A small group of figures were staggering across it – matchstick shapes from this distance, but Dora recognised the tattered black clothes and black mop-hair of Sophie, who was only covering the rugged ground at the speed she was because a tall young man, presumably Andrei, was propping her up. The group was clearly in the last stage of exhaustion; instead of using the cover of the ruins, they were tottering along in the open. About fifty metres behind them, three more figures – clad in body-armour and hunting fatigues – capered in pursuit. However, these surviving members of the hunting party only discharged the occasional bolt, and seemed to be deliberately missing their targets, striking the ground or flattening nearby buildings, as if herding the terrified humans. They laughed excitedly.

'They're enjoying themselves, aren't they?' the Doctor said grimly.

'Do something, please!'

The Doctor was thinking quickly, but no obvious solution presented itself. At the far side of the wasteland was the upward curved perimeter of the dome wall, though at this point it adjoined with a different dome: an immense arched entranceway giving through to another set of towering, rusted structures – almost certainly the rocket base. It was difficult to see clearly through the stained and misted partition, but one particular tower over there, a huge flimsy edifice, soared above all the others. That had to be the base control tower, which was a reassuring sight, though it was at least a couple of miles away from here, and not only did he have to get himself and Dora over there in one piece, but he had to get the other fugitives there as well.

A change in tone from the hunters caught his attention. He peered down. They had halted, and seemed to be milling around in a minor panic. Finally, they took cover behind the skeleton of an earth-mover.

Very slowly, the Doctor smiled.

'What's happening?' Dora asked.

'They're getting a dose of their own medicine,' he said. 'They're taking fire.'

Chapter
31

Rory and Harry bawled with laughter as the hunters went to ground.

Rory loaded another hunk of rock onto his catapult and let fly. The missile winged its way across the ruins, and struck the caterpillar track behind which the crown of a hunter's helmet had just ducked. He and Harry were perched inside the scoop of a derelict crane. Its jib was partly lowered, so they'd been able to scramble up it, and had found it an excellent vantage point from which to assail the enemy with the array of primitive weapons they'd brought from the labour camp. As well as Rory's catapult, for which he had a stockpile of ammunition, Harry had a homemade crossbow, and a quiver full of flint-tipped arrows. They also had a spear and a sling.

Harry discharged another arrow. Rory let fly with another lump of rock. The hunters had only been about fifty metres away when they'd come under attack, so the first few shots had struck cleanly. Now they'd taken cover and were all but invisible, but Rory and Harry kept up their bombardment, determined to buy as much time for the fleeing fugitives as they could.

'Having a good time up there?' someone called from below.

Rory glanced down, and saw the Doctor and Dora standing on the ground beneath them. The Doctor's arms were folded. He was smiling, but sternly – like a lecturer just about tolerating amusing but wayward behaviour from his students.

'Doctor!' Rory laughed delightedly. 'I knew you'd get here! Look – we've got them pinned down!'

'So I see,' the Doctor replied. From ground level, it was impossible to pinpoint where the hunting party had hidden themselves, but he knew they wouldn't lie low indefinitely. 'I take it you're not alone?'

'He certainly is not,' Harry said, poking his head out of the jib. 'I'll have you know this was my idea – *Dora!*'

'*Harry!*' she screamed.

Harry made to scramble back down the jib, but Rory stopped him. 'We need to maintain this assault. The longer we keep them—'

'The longer you maintain this assault, Rory,' the Doctor shouted, 'the more likely they are to locate your exact position. And remember, each one of those men has a weapon that can turn this machine into a pile of tooth fillings.'

Rory and Harry hurriedly clambered down. Harry and Dora embraced for several seconds, before he stepped backwards and regarded her outfit.

'I like the new look,' he said.

'Well… it's practical,' she replied.

'You remind me of Lara Croft.'

'Don't be daft.'

Harry glanced towards the Doctor, wondering who he was. It might have been his imagination, but Rory, who'd been a life-saver so far, suddenly seemed less authoritative in this young stranger's presence.

'I'm… well, you know… sorry,' Rory was in the middle of saying.

'The deep and lasting recriminations can come later,' the Doctor replied. 'At the moment, I suspect we're about to have company.'

They peered through the ruins, and saw three figures bobbing up and down as they moved from one hiding place to the next, steadily encroaching.

The Doctor spun into action. 'Rory, you and Harry hold them off. Dora, come with me.'

The two men brandished their makeshift weapons as they took up firing positions behind a pile of empty oil drums.

'Where are we going?' Dora said, following the Doctor to the rear of the crane.

'Fancy a drive?'

'What?'

Behind the massive machine, there was yet another heap of junk: more oil drums, more layers of broken panelling.

'Where are we going to get a car?' she asked.

'How about… *here*!' He stripped debris from the mound, and revealed the skeletal chassis of a squat, squarish vehicle, the interior of which had been completely burned out. It had no doors, no windows. Its wheels were circles of bare metal. But the Doctor looked pleased.

'An Outskirter Buggy. Ideal. These are the workhorses of Torodon heavy industry. Designed for personnel transport, haulage, you name it.'

'But it's got no tyres.'

'I only said we were going for a drive. I didn't say it would be smooth.'

'It's got no seats in it, either.'

'Or comfortable.' He moved around to the front. 'All we really need is an engine.'

When he tried to lift the bonnet, it came away in his hands. This didn't stop him poking around underneath, though he was briefly distracted when an energy bolt impacted close by. 'That isn't good. We can probably outrun those bored businessmen, but not their gunfire. Got to get this thing working.'

Dora gazed in at the engine, if that was what it was – it was more a confusion of conduits, valves and cables, all jammed in around a central block-like structure, which was covered with a fine, plasticky resin.

'The solenoids appear to be intact,' the Doctor muttered. 'Excellent. The heads and terminals undamaged. Even better. The cabling and relays are still connected to the ignition switch.' He tapped a forefinger on the central block. 'Battery looks almost as good as new.'

'That's a battery?' Dora said.

'Outskirter Buggies are always electrical. Unusually far-sighted of the Torodon – their industries are generally filthy.'

There was another explosive impact. Dora rushed to the corner of the crane, and saw that Rory and Harry had had to change position, though they were still returning fire. The barrier of oil drums had been blown apart, and there was smoke everywhere.

'Doctor, hurry!' she cried, running back.

'Almost done,' he replied.

He'd taken out his sonic screwdriver, unscrewed its base and extracted a long, silvery core with a crystal bauble attached to either end. He now loosened the two baubles, swapped them around and carefully reinserted the core, before snapping the tool back together. 'Now... we've no insulation material, so there'll be sparks.'

Dora stepped back as he held the screwdriver within touching distance of a copper wire coiled tightly into a helix. There was, as he'd forecast, a flash, followed by a jarring CRUNCH of gears – and the engine rumbled to life.

'You did it!' Dora cried. 'That device is incredible.'

The Doctor shoved the screwdriver back into his pocket. 'I've said it before and I'll say it again – no one must ever dis the sonic.' He dashed round to the driver's door. 'But this won't last long. Perhaps give us a mile before the power cells burn out. Come on.'

When the battered, burned-out wreck pulled up behind Rory and Harry, they could only rise from their concealed positions agog.

'Someone order a taxi?' the Doctor asked.

Chapter
32

One by one, the three hunters emerged through the smog of dust left behind the Outskirter. One by one, they lowered their weapons.

Their names were Zargoz, Krillig and Klyber, and they were respectively a stockbroker, a banker and the managing director of a successful sports and retail giant. All of them were dustier and more bedraggled than they would normally be at this stage on a 'fun hunt'. One of the lenses in Klyber's goggles had been knocked out by a catapulted rock, rendering his long-range visualiser defunct. A crossbow bolt was buried between two of Zargoz's shoulder-plates. Its flint tip had drawn blood from the flesh beneath.

They watched the rapidly dwindling buggy for several seconds. Only then did Krillig notice the figure on the ridge behind them. It was Xorg Krauzzen, elevated to a metre in the air on his hover-plate and carrying a photon-rifle across his shoulder. His attention was also fixed on the escaping vehicle, which was now little more than a dot. More of Krauzzen's men appeared, slogging on foot, but all carrying photon-weapons. Krauzzen glided slowly down from the ridge.

'Pity you weren't here a few minutes ago,' Klyber said petulantly. 'We were under attack. In danger.'

Krauzzen gazed towards the horizon, his wax-smooth face unmarked by emotion.

'They only had primitive weapons,' Zargoz said. 'But they were effective at short range. It gave them an opportunity to elude us. I've been hurt, by the way. It's only a nick, but I hope your medical bay has a suitable antibiotic. I don't want to come down with some ghastly blood infection.'

Krauzzen focused on the skeletal structures of the rocket base, which were just visible in the next dome.

'None of us called you, Krauzzen,' Krillig said. 'I hope you don't think this means the hunt is over?'

Krauzzen responded by turning his hover-plate around and cruising several metres to one side. He nodded to his men.

Their photon-rifles rose in unison.

'Wait!' Zargoz shouted. '*What is this?*'

The gangsters opened fire, blowing the three hunters to the ground, where they blasted them over and over until they were nothing but embers and smoking ash.

About a mile and a half away, the Doctor's ramshackle transport ground to a halt alongside a crater, where Sophie, Andrei and the other exhausted fugitives had been lying low, gasping for breath. Dora was now too busy hugging the weeping Sophie to notice the distant cacophony of gunfire. Harry was too busy pumping Andrei's hand and clapping his shoulder in gratitude for keeping their daughter alive. The other fugitives were preoccupied by the mobile heap of junk their rescuers had arrived in; they watched in awe as its one remaining section of bodywork dropped off.

Of them all, only Rory glanced back through the ruins.

'For some reason, I don't like the sound of that,' he said.

'Me neither,' the Doctor agreed, though he declined to voice what he suspected it meant. 'All aboard everyone. You can promise never to hurt each other again later.'

The fugitives crammed into the buggy, which jolted and creaked as it struggled on across the broken ground. The Doctor wasn't particularly enjoying driving it. The gears jammed constantly, and the sponge that had once upholstered the steering wheel only remained in sticky, charred stubs. However, the Outskirter was still capable of movement, which was more than he'd expected.

The dome containing the rocket base was more severely damaged than the others. A large section of its roof was retractable, to allow for the arrival and departure of spacecraft, but this was now frozen open, so the acid rain poured through in torrents. Where certain of the launch buildings and pads had once been located, there were nothing but blistered ruins, still smoking and hissing as the caustic fluid continued to eat its way through them. Thick billows of corrosive steam blew across the site.

'Just breathing this air is making my throat sore,' Dora said, as the Doctor wove the rickety vehicle amid the rotting structures.

'There's sufficient wind from the outside to prevent these emissions building to a fatal level,' the Doctor replied. 'But the atmosphere's severely tainted. You'd get better quality of life on a landfill.'

Ahead of them loomed the control tower. It was a monumental edifice, at least sixty metres high, constructed from steel girders and with a discus-shaped superstructure at its apex.

'You want us to climb *that*?' Rory said.

'We haven't got any choice,' the Doctor replied. 'The most powerful radio transmitter on Gorgoror may still be at the top.'

'*May* still be?'

'Let's not worry ourselves with semantics.'

A few metres further on, the Outskirter sputtered to an undignified halt, one of its wheels rolling away as it clattered down onto its shocks.

The Doctor climbed out and observed the tower. A stairway spiralled up its central core, but was likely to be rusted to the bone. Briefly, he had second thoughts. It might have been safer to leave everyone else down here, and go up there alone – but in truth there was nowhere here for them to hide.

'And if we're all up there, what's to stop Krauzzen blowing it up?' Harry asked.

'Curiosity,' the Doctor said, hands thrust in his pockets.

'How do you mean?'

'Well, if I were him, I'd want to know who it was who scuppered his plans, who managed to start the engine of a car that's been dead for thirty years—'

'You think he might be impressed?'

'Krauzzen exists outside Torodon law. Just to survive, he needs to make the best of every situation. After this, I doubt he'll be holding any more fun hunts here, so he has to walk away with some kind of prize.' The Doctor turned, and saw the rest of the fugitives gathered around him. They were a little fresher, having driven the last few miles, but they still looked strained and haggard. 'A quick climb and everything will be hunky dory,' he said cheerfully.

'I thought you didn't believe in lying to people?' Rory mumbled.

'Did I say that? Maybe I was fibbing. Don't worry. We're not finished yet,' the Doctor replied.

Climbing the control tower was every bit as nerve-wracking as they'd expected. The buildings around its base were hollowed shells, but the stair, which they accessed single file from a central courtyard, was intact – at least at its lower section. However, the higher they rose the more the structure felt as if it was swaying. There were endless groans and creaks. They encountered segments of stair where the hand-rail had broken or corroded, and where even the risers were loose. Rory glanced down across the rocket base, but the billows of steam only afforded him brief glimpses of the arched entrance from the neighbouring dome, and as yet there was no sign of anyone coming through it.

About thirty metres up, there was a viewing deck: a narrow, railed catwalk which circled the tower's exterior. Sixty metres away on a level with this was the roof of the next nearest building. They'd noticed this before – from ground level it was nothing more than an immense, square concrete box, with almost no windows or other distinguishing features. But from this vantage point, they saw that its upper surface was bristling with antennae and parabolic reflector dishes. The Doctor moved to the edge of the viewing deck, to stare more closely at it.

'Now,' he said. 'Big windowless thingy with everything happening on top. Couldn't be a Solar Transduction Centre by any chance? Yes, of course it could.'

'What's a Solar Transduction Centre?' Rory asked.

'Hopefully something we won't need. In a nutshell, that's a giant transducer. Would've been used as back-up in the event of Gorgoror's nuclear reactor being deactivated. It would literally have run this entire complex on stored solar energy.' The Doctor rubbed his chin. 'There could be decades' worth of power still latent in there. The trouble is we're over *here*.'

'You mean we've got to go back down?'

'Nope. No time for that.'

'I've just looked and I didn't see anyone following us.'

'You won't see them until it's too late.'

'But if there's no power…?'

The Doctor glanced back down the stairway. The others were clattering wearily up, but trailing below to a distance of twelve metres. It would be impossible to pass them all until they'd reached this viewing deck, and that would take even more minutes that couldn't be spared.

'Never mind.' He started up the next flight. 'The control deck may have a battery reserve in case of power failure.'

'That's a heck of a gamble,' Rory said, following.

'They've all paid off so far.'

The control deck – the discus-shaped capsule they'd

seen from below – was about twenty metres in diameter and, in appearance, resembled a flying saucer, with viewing ports around its outer bulkhead. It was perched on the very top of the tower, with another viewing deck directly below it from which a single set of step-ladders led up through a hatch into its interior – which had quite literally been trashed.

Rory viewed the mess with dismay.

There were control boards everywhere, bashed in or torn loose. Cables, circuitry and other computer innards strewed the floor in a spaghetti-like muddle. What looked like a radio console, though it was more complex than any Rory had ever seen, had been beaten as though with blunt instruments. Again, its delicate contents had disgorged in a chaotic deluge.

'Well,' Rory said. 'That's that.'

The Doctor shook his head. 'Not quite. I'd say there were enough spare parts lying around in here for us to lash something together.'

The rest of the fugitives filed up one by one. They weren't sure what they'd been expecting to find in here. Something in the Doctor's air of authority had encouraged them that, once they'd made it to this eagle's nest, all their problems would be solved. They stood, breathing heavily, mopping sweat, watching the Doctor scamper about, grabbing up odds and ends.

'What's happening now?' Harry whispered to Rory.

'He's lashing something together.'

'Like what – a magic wand?'

Dora elbowed her husband in the side. 'He got that car going, didn't he?'

The Doctor suddenly noticed that he had an audience.

He smiled. 'I don't always operate well under scrutiny. Why don't you all go below and keep a lookout?'

Obediently, they descended to the viewing deck. Soon only Rory was left, gazing bemused as the Doctor quickly and systematically cannibalised the wreckage in the room, assembling entirely new mechanisms from the broken fragments littering the floor, weaving the ends of shredded cables together, stripping insulation material away with his teeth, and looping the metal threads around his fingers and thumbs to create entirely new lines of circuits and contacts.

When Rory finally went below, the rest of them were spread around the viewing deck, peering into the encircling gulf.

'What's the next step?' Harry asked.

Rory shrugged. 'We wait.'

'If it comes to a fight, you can rely on me,' someone said.

Andrei had stepped forward, Sophie still clinging to his arm.

'That's good to know,' Rory said, trying his best to look upbeat.

This guy Andrei would be a useful bloke to have around in most situations, but he probably had no idea what they were up against here. They'd so far survived by the skin of their teeth, and even the Doctor seemed to be making things up as he went along. Whatever he was trying to do at present seemed utterly futile.

'This is an urgent message from Gorgoror Moon,' came the Doctor's voice from overhead. 'We are in grave peril, and require immediate assistance. Over.'

Rory rushed back upstairs, to find the Doctor sitting

in the midst of reconstructed clutter, attempting to speak into a microphone, which looked as if he'd patched it together with sticky tape.

'I repeat, we require urgent assistance…'

There was no response. Not even the hiss of dead air.

By the look on the Doctor's face, Rory felt his newly rekindled hopes diminish.

'No power,' the Doctor finally said. 'None left in any of these circuits, and no reserve supply… at least not up here.' He glanced at Rory. 'I'm afraid this gamble has failed.'

Chapter
33

'You should know, there's no way out of here!' Zarbotan said loudly, as he roved from aisle to aisle. 'I've jammed the lock on the door, so the access-card you stole is no longer viable.' His hover-plate made no sound as he glided past one row of stacked shelves after another. 'I see you sprang that fool Xorax from confinement. That's another black mark against you. Siding with Lord Krauzzen's enemies makes no sense, and will avail you nothing. This is your last chance, girl. Show yourself voluntarily, save me further trouble, and I'll simply return you to duty. But keep me busy in here, and when I finally find you – and I will – I'll give you first to Xaaael, and what's left of you after that to Madam Xagra. Neither are your friends at this moment.'

Amy listened in growing terror. She'd scurried from one hiding place to the next, but none had proved adequate. Any tarpaulins covering items of cargo were bound or stapled into place. None of the boxes or crates she'd so far tried had lids that she could prise off. A couple of times she tried to double back on herself by climbing back through one of the stacks – yet Zarbotan seemed to possess an unerring sense of where she was. He was slowly but surely herding her across the Secure Hold into an open corner where, beyond a hexagonal-shaped aperture, a passage ramped downward into dimness. The last thing Amy wanted to do was bolt down a rabbit hole and find herself trapped, but nothing else suggested itself.

When she finally descended the ramp, it ended, as she'd feared, in a low, vault-like chamber. She pivoted around, trying to work out her next move. The place was jammed with discarded rubbish – the splintered shells of jemmied-open crates, empty metal containers, torn sacking, bundles of paper packaging. There were control panels everywhere, giving off a low hum and dull lighting, but it was anyone's guess what their purpose was. At the far end of the room, set into a central portion of the floor, was a circular hatch, a little over a metre in diameter. It was made from some shiny, ceramic material, and fixed in place with a steel collar. There was no obvious way to open it. It had no handle or buttons. When Amy stamped on it, it didn't give.

Zarbotan's voice drifted down the ramp towards her. 'You've had your chance, girl. My patience has run out.'

With heavy clanks of his semi-mechanical feet, he descended.

Frantic, Amy dug her way through the refuse, drawing sheets of bubble-wrap over her head. She caught a last glimpse of Zarbotan as he strode into view. He'd inserted the hover-plate into a harness buckled to his back, and had drawn his photon-pistol. With practised malevolence, he raised it until his arm was ramrod-straight and moved slowly from one pile of rubbish to the next. His aim came to rest on a torpedo-shaped container, the open door to which revealed an empty interior. He fired, and a pulse of blinding light shot into the container, blasting it apart and then folding it up into a smouldering, semi-liquid knot.

'Just imagine the effect of that on your soft human flesh,' he laughed.

He now took pot-shots around the vault. There were thunderous impacts. Fountains of scorched and shattered rubbish exploded into the air. Amy scuttled beneath the debris like a rat, but finally she was cornered. A thin cork hoarding was all she could shelter beneath, and Zarbotan ripped it away.

Amy cowered as he stood over her. There was no mercy in his bisected face. The 'living' section scowled; the 'dead' section was blank.

She saw his grip tighten on the pistol's hilt, and screwed her eyes shut.

The next sound she heard, however, was not the squeal of discharged energy, but a deep *CLUNK* of metal, followed by Zarbotan's brief, angry shout.

When Amy's eyes snapped open again, he was no longer there.

But she wasn't alone.

Xorax had reappeared, and was standing by the entrance. One of his hands was clamped on a polished brass instrument, which looked distinctly like a lever. Confused, she glanced further around the room – and her eyes came to rest on the point where Zarbotan had just been standing – on the circular ceramic hatchway, which was now irising closed.

Amy climbed to her feet. 'What... how?'

'Joining forces with Krauzzen's enemies will avail you something,' Xorax said with grim satisfaction. 'Survival.'

'But where is he?'

Xorax beckoned her. When she joined him, he stepped aside and tapped a crystal scope. She gazed into it, and it was as though she was staring down a narrow tube. At the far end, very distant, she could see the streaming turmoil of Gorgoror's upper atmosphere. A tiny figure was plummeting through it, pin-wheeling.

'Down the garbage chute,' Xorax replied. 'Where he belongs!'

Chapter
34

'**Andrei has an idea,**' Rory said.

The Doctor was preoccupied with the heap of disordered cable and circuitry which he was still trying to breathe life into. He surveyed it distractedly, his mind racing through one possible solution after another.

'Doctor… ?'

The Doctor turned to find Rory, Harry and Andrei on the control deck with him.

'You say the building opposite is some kind of energy store?' Andrei said. 'Is it a simple matter of reactivating the power source in that building?'

'Well, it's not *that* simple,' the Doctor replied. 'The Solar Transduction Centre would re-energise the entire complex. It would give us all the power we need, but Krauzzen and his cronies are still lurking around down there somewhere. Probably the only thing holding them at bay is fear of my transmat-rifle.'

'Transmat-rifle?' Rory said.

'It doesn't matter. I've lost it anyway. The point is that whoever tries to climb back down this tower will never be climbing up it again.'

'What if we were to *slide* over there?' Andrei said.

The Doctor appraised him. 'How do you mean.'

Andrei raised Harry's crossbow. 'I can fire a zip-line across to the roof of the Transduction Centre. Someone could slide down it.'

The Doctor pondered this, before hurrying down the ladder to the platform beneath. The rest of the fugitives moved aside as he stood by the barrier facing the Transduction Centre. The distance to the ground was immense, and, aside from a great mound of ash and cinders mid-way across, mostly it was cluttered with piles of razor-edged scrap. Not only that, the angle of descent would be perilous. Whoever slid down the line would be travelling at terrific speed.

'No one's attempted to scale the tower yet?' he asked over his shoulder.

'Not yet,' Dora replied.

'It might work. Just.' He hurried back up to the control deck, reappearing seconds later with several bits and pieces, and a coil of flexible, high-tensile twine. 'This stuff was part of an escape kit, in case the tower ever became unstable. The twine looks thin, but don't be fooled. It's designed to bear extreme loads.'

'Well, that's the zip-line taken care of,' Rory said, 'but how are we going to anchor it on the Transduction Centre roof?'

'Nothing simpler,' the Doctor replied. 'What missiles have we got?'

Harry handed over a small bundle of makeshift

arrows. None was especially aerodynamic, but so long as they flew and could at least hit a large target they would suffice. Even better, one had a brass eyelet set into its base.

The Doctor fingered it. 'We'll use this one. But first we loop the twine through it, so we'll have a double line. We then haul *this* over there.' He produced a small but sturdy grappling hook. 'This should find a secure grip. All we need do then is fasten the line at this end, and I'll be ready.'

'*You'll* be ready?' Rory said.

The Doctor shrugged. 'I think I deserve some of the fun, don't you? Anyway, does anyone else here know how to reactivate a Solar Transduction Centre?'

'No one else knows how to operate a homemade Torodon radio set either,' Rory said. 'If you get killed doing this, the rest of us are trapped up here.'

The Doctor glanced from Rory to Harry to Andrei, unable to deny this logic. 'OK, good point there.'

'Can't you just tell one of us what to do?' Andrei said. 'Write it down, maybe?'

The Doctor scrubbed a hand through his mop of hair. 'It may not be too complicated. There could even be a breaker-switch in the Emergency Maintenance Shed, which will be that domed structure in the very middle of the roof.'

'What would this breaker-switch look like?' Harry asked.

The Doctor shrugged. 'Just that – a switch or lever. Probably behind a sheet of tempered glass, to protect it. But a device simple enough for a low-grade maintenance tech to operate.' He moved back to the parapet. 'Whatever, we'll have to move fast. I imagine Krauzzen's men are pretty good shots – they've had enough practice.'

With the twine fitted to the arrow, Andrei took aim. He struck the roof easily, but the arrow ricocheted off a reflector dish and slid across its bitumen-like surface, finally coming to a standstill. Andrei lugged it back, only for the shaft to wedge itself across two horizontal struts. The line went taut.

Rory hooked the grapple to the line, and released it. It slid down across the gulf, hitting the rooftop barrier with a dull clank.

'Easy does it,' the Doctor said.

With gentle tugs and manipulations, they worked the grapple over the barrier, and yanked on it hard, snapping it into place. The zip-line felt secure.

'First class!' the Doctor shouted. 'Well done everyone!'

They tied the line to one of the steel bars overarching the viewing deck, and the only thing then was to decide who would be making the one-way trip.

'You're needed here, Doctor,' Rory argued. 'That's why I should go.'

'I can't allow that,' Andrei put in. 'It was my idea. I should go.'

'You understand just how dangerous this is going to be?' the Doctor said.

'But it's our only chance,' Rory replied.

'Perhaps we should draw lots for it,' Andrei said. 'But not you, Doctor.'

Rory agreed. 'Definitely not you.'

'*Daddy!*' Sophie shrieked.

They spun around, and saw that Harry had removed

his jacket, looped it over the zip-line, and was standing on top of the barrier. 'Age and ugliness before beauty and usefulness!' he said with a grin.

'Harry, wait!' the Doctor shouted.

But Harry had leapt from the platform and was already sailing down across the gulf.

Krauzzen tracked Harry's progress through the super-powered electroscope on his photon-rifle. He was still at ground level, but concealed in one of the base's ruined outbuildings. His minions were gathered around him, wondering why he didn't fire. Harry had almost completed his crossing when Krauzzen lowered his rifle.

'Let's see what they come up with,' he said.

'Shouldn't we at least advance on the tower?' someone asked.

'He'd pick us all off before we'd crossed the open ground.' Krauzzen shouldered his weapon. 'Be patient. I'm interested to see just how deep this Doctor's ingenuity goes.'

Chapter
35

Harry struck the barrier on the edge of the Transduction Centre roof with bone-rattling force, but managed to hang on and got his legs over the parapet. When he stood up, he looked shaken by the impact, but staggered away towards the Emergency Maintenance Shed. Dora and Sophie hugged each other with relief, and then cheered loudly, urging him on. Harry glanced back and waved, before struggling to slide his bulk through the dome's narrow aperture.

Once inside, he was gone for several minutes. They watched from the tower in silence. There was a shrill but muffled clattering – as of something being struck.

'The glass case over the breaker-switch,' the Doctor said. 'He's trying to smash his way in. That won't be easy.'

Clearly it wasn't, because several more, painfully long minutes passed, before there was a sudden silence. Everyone held their breath, not sure what to expect.

And then the Doctor smiled and pointed.

Half a mile away, a set of runway lights were gleaming through the drifting murk. Other lights began flickering to life. There was a sudden hum of electricity, and the hiss of a valve being released. A puff of flame appeared from a nearby stack of pipes. From the distance, came the repeated echoing of a klaxon.

That was when they heard the voice of Amy Pond.

'Doctor, this is Amy... are you receiving me? I repeat, are you receiving me?'

The Doctor dashed for the ladder. On the control deck, he found his lashed-together radio set aglow with power.

'Hello, Amy,' he shouted into its transmitter. 'This is the Doctor, receiving.'

'Where have you been?' Her voice turned cross. 'I've been trying you for ages.'

'Sorry about that. We've had a few ups and downs.'

'Fine, whatever... now can you please just get us out of this?'

'I'm afraid you're going to have to get yourself out of this one, Amy. And us.'

There was a brief, static-filled silence.

'What?' Amy said finally.

'There's nothing I can do for you without the TARDIS. So you'll need to pilot it down here.'

'This is a joke, yeah?'

'And as we're about sixty metres above the ground, and your target area is roughly twenty metres by twenty, a precision landing will be nine points of the law. Though that shouldn't be too difficult because you can home in on my sonic screwdriver. Oh... always assuming the frequency isn't being scrambled by Torodon interplanetary satellites. In which case, you'll need to bypass the electromagnetic spectrum, and feed the—'

'*Doctor, just stop!* You know I've never flown the TARDIS.'

'Now's not the time for nit-picking, Amelia.'

'This is madness.'

'Or a touch of genius. We'll know one way or the other very soon. Now pay attention, because I'll be giving you precise instructions.'

'I hope you know what you're doing.'

'Have you ever known anyone more in control of himself in times of crisis?'

'You don't really want me to answer that question, do you?'

'Possibly not. Now…' He was about to issue directives, when he heard Amy talking to someone else, apparently trying to reassure whoever it was that they were safe inside the TARDIS – despite a furious banging and crashing on its door.

'Amy, who is that with you?'

'What? Oh, some bloke called Xorax.'

'Xorax? A Torodon?'

'He's a prisoner I released.'

'Krauzzen was holding a fellow Torodon prisoner?' the Doctor asked.

'Does it matter? I'll make sure he doesn't touch anything…'

'*Listen!*' Suddenly, the Doctor had to struggle to keep the excitement from his voice. 'Keep this Xorax with you. At all costs, don't lose him.'

'And where am I going to lose him to?'

'Don't be flippant, Pond. And listen carefully. It's

not every day I give a crash course in trans-dimensional navigation.'

Rory listened tensely, hoping Amy understood more of what the Doctor said next than he did. He vaguely recognised some of the terms – 'in-flight stabiliser', 'time-flow regulator', 'space-directional modulator' – because he'd heard the Doctor mention them while busying around the TARDIS console, but in reality they might have been a foreign language. He was distracted by sounds of cheering from below.

He scrambled down the ladder and joined the others.

Lights were now visible all over the spaceport and even beyond, in the neighbouring domes. Steam vented from outflow pipes on the Transduction Centre roof. A reflector dish was rotating on its axis. However, the cheers were for Harry, who was limping back towards the parapet. When he reached it, he placed one hand on his belly, and bowed solemnly.

He never saw the other figure rise into view a few metres away from him.

Even if he had, he wouldn't have recognised the short, squat figure of Colonel Xon Krelbin. The Colonel's black vinyl fatigues were rent and torn, and glistened with blood; his face was so beaten and clawed that it was a miracle he was on his feet at all. But he was, and he was now levelling a rifle at Harry's back. Rory shouted a hoarse warning. The others shouted too. It all came too late. A searing beam of energy struck Harry full on. He froze, before vanishing in a blaze of blue light.

*

On the control deck, the Doctor only half-heard the consternation below. He'd given Amy sufficient data to programme the TARDIS, and had now made a much longer-range transmission, contacting the Main Police Despatch Centre on LP9. From that point on it had become *really* difficult.

'Look,' he said, infuriated. 'I wouldn't be using this channel if I was a prank caller. I need to speak to Police Chief Zalu, and I need to speak to him right now.'

The despatch officer replied again that his commander did not take personal calls.

'Does this sound like a personal call?' the Doctor snapped. 'Do I sound like I'm trying to arrange a boys' night out?'

Rory clambered up into view. He gestured at the Doctor, who tried to wave him away.

'Harry's just been killed!' Rory blurted.

The Doctor went cold. 'What… how?'

'One of the hunters climbed up to the roof and shot him. Disintegrated him.'

The Doctor could still hear the despatch officer spouting negatives into his ear, and now responded angrily. 'Listen, I may be cut off any moment now. In fact we may be about to lose all power here, so please think about this very carefully: would I have patched myself through to the heart of your classified network if I didn't (a) have astonishing abilities which are surely worthy of investigation, and (b) have information for Chief Zalu of quite staggering importance?'

There was a brief silence, before the officer asked: 'What is this information?'

'Tell him that Krauzzen…' The Doctor paused on

hearing an intake of breath. 'That's right... tell him that *Xorg Krauzzen* is holding a Torodon national against his will, and threatening to having him executed. Did you get—'

The radio went dead. All over the complex, lights faded and died. Klaxons fell silent. Steam ceased to pour from vents.

With no other option, the Doctor followed Rory down to the viewing deck.

Andrei, rather awkwardly, was attempting to comfort Dora and Sophie, who clutched each other and wept. The rest of the fugitives regarded them with woe-stricken faces. A jeering voice drew the Doctor's attention to the Transduction Centre roof, where the battered shape of Colonel Krelbin had re-emerged from the Emergency Maintenance Shed and now stood on the parapet, holding his knife aloft in one hand and, in the other, what looked like a shock of blood-streaked hair. At first, the Doctor had the horrible notion this might be Harry's scalp, but then remembered Rory saying that Harry had been disintegrated.

In some ways it was even more disconcerting to realise that this scalp had once belonged to the monstrous shologgi.

Down in the ruins, Krauzzen and his men watched with fascination.

'That's Krelbin?' one of them said.

Krauzzen nodded. 'And that weapon he just used is not his own. Damn it, it's the Doctor's Obliterator! Which means we're clear to attack. All of you, *now!*'

*

'Doctor!' Andrei said. 'Our enemy are closing.'

The Doctor saw hunched figures, photon-rifles levelled as they scuttled across the waste ground.

'That's not our only problem,' Rory said, pointing along the zip-line.

Krelbin had sheathed his knife, shouldered his rifle, and was hanging by his hands and knees as he worked his way across.

'Not to worry,' the Doctor said. 'Amy's on her way.'

Hopefully none of them noticed that he had his fingers crossed behind his back. She'd listened to his instructions attentively, but learning to fly a TARDIS, even along a pre-programmed route, was not something you generally picked up in two minutes.

Chapter
36

After immersion in the blue flare, Harry went spinning through a glittering vortex, during the course of which he became unconscious. When he opened his eyes again, he was lying on the floor in a bare ten-by-ten room, with a foil blanket laid over him.

That had been a quarter of an hour ago. Now he was sitting up, groggy. A tall, severe looking and yet rather handsome Torodon woman watched from the doorway. She was dressed in a tight-fitting uniform made from shiny, silvery-blue material.

Harry tried to smile at her, but still felt queasy. She didn't return the smile, and he noticed that she was holding a punch-stick.

He was about to speak, when an older Torodon male entered. He was bald and thickly moustached. He too wore a tight, silver-blue uniform, but didn't fill it as well. He folded his arms as he appraised Harry. 'I apologise that there's no bed for you to recover on,' he finally said, 'but the last creature the Doctor sent here dissolved it.'

Harry felt a jolt of hope. 'You know the Doctor?'

'If only I didn't.'

'Who are you people?'

The twosome glanced at each other, puzzled.

'Has he been given a full medical?' the male asked.

'The FMO looked him over,' the female replied. 'He's in reasonable shape.'

The male turned back to Harry. 'Can you stand up?'

Harry levered himself to his feet. He still felt weak and disoriented, but his strength was returning. He didn't notice how torn and filthy his clothes were, or how many deep gashes had dribbled blood onto them.

But Kobal Zalu did. He bit his lip as the reality of what these people were going through struck him. 'How is it up there?' he asked.

'Up there?'

'On Gorgoror.'

Harry ran fingers through his damp, dirty hair. 'Chaos. We're being hunted, murdered. The Doctor was trying to help us.'

Zalu looked even more discomforted. He turned and left the room. The female followed

'Wait!' Harry lurched dizzily after them. 'Are you some kind of police force? Hey, you can at least answer my questions.'

The small room opened not into a cell corridor as Harry had expected, but into a large, octagonal chamber. The room was in fact a tank on a raised dais, with various pipes and insulated cables feeding into it. Another Torodon, a younger male, operated a freestanding bank of controls.

Zalu turned to face Harry. 'You're in the LP9 Police HQ. You're safe here. You can rest, bathe, eat. But you've got to keep out of our way, especially mine. I'm too busy to talk to civilians.'

'I'm not a civilian,' Harry said. 'I'm a cop. Like you.'

Again, the police chief glanced at his female colleague. This time there was clear surprise on their faces – along with something else: uncertainty, concern.

'You're here on duty?' the female asked.

'Well… no. But I was carrying out an investigation when I was abducted.'

There was a long silence. The woman looked questioningly at her superior. He stiffened, before shaking his head. 'I'm sorry about that,' he said. 'But you've no jurisdiction here. And I couldn't help you, even if I wanted to.'

'Which means you *don't* want to?' Harry said. 'Look, what kind of people are you? You call yourselves police, yet there are folk being murdered and you're just hanging around here in your office?'

The officers again exchanged discomforted looks, before Zalu spun around and strode for a slide-door, which shot open to admit him.

'We respect that you're police officer,' the woman said. 'But you're from Earth. You can't understand the political dimensions we have to cope with here.'

'Politics!' Harry laughed. 'Are you kidding? I know all about politics. It's turned the job upside down. On Earth, we had to fight crime with one hand tied behind our back. We still fought it, though. What's your chief's name?'

'That was Chief Officer of Police Zalu, and he's very busy.'

Before she could stop him, Harry ran for the same slide-door. It shot open, and beyond it there was a small compartment.

'Top floor!' he shouted, more by instinct than logic.

The door slid closed before the woman could step in with him, and he ascended, coming to a halt again in a high-tech office filled with plasma screens on which images and data played rapidly. Numerous Torodon police officers moved around. Harry pressed through them, until he saw his target in mid-discussion with someone.

'Chief Zalu!' Harry shouted.

Heads switched towards him, astonished. Zalu raised a bushy white eyebrow.

'Whatever evidence you need, you've got it,' Harry said, approaching. 'I'm a walking, talking witness statement. I'm not scared of this guy Krauzzen. I'll stand up in court, testify against him. I won't crack under the interrogation of some mob lawyer.'

'If only it was that simple,' Zalu said gruffly.

'Hey, we have a phrase on Earth. Not everyone likes it, but it was pretty universal when I joined the job. It goes: "We're the cops; we can do anything."'

'Congratulations,' Zalu replied. 'When you finally return to this police state you call home, give my condolences to the law-abiding citizens who have to suffer under it.' And he strode away, vanishing through another slide-door.

Harry noticed that the tall female officer had joined them.

'Is he a law officer or not?' he asked.

'Of course he's a law officer,' she retorted. 'He's one

of the best.'

'Did he not understand what I just said?'

'He understood. But while you have to fight crime with one hand tied behind your back, there are times when we have both tied behind ours.'

'Even when it comes to murder, kidnapping?'

'I'm afraid so.'

'You Torodon have got some pretty strange ideas.'

'You're telling *me* that?' she said. 'I'm a woman.'

Harry bustled on through the room, entered a narrow passage, which gave through to various other offices. He heard the female calling for him to stop, but for some reason she didn't follow him. At the end of the passage, he found a smaller office in which three male officers were seated behind consoles. Zalu was disappearing through a door on the other side.

'Yo!' Harry shouted, again dashing through before anyone could stop him.

Zalu had just slumped behind his desk. He looked thoroughly exasperated by the ongoing intrusion.

'Listen,' Harry said, 'there was a time when I was a lazy cop, too.'

Zalu's eyebrows arched. 'What's that?'

'I admit I made a hash of my police career. I got bored, I got silly. I was taking the perks and not delivering the service, you know what I mean?'

'I've tried to tell you that I'm too busy—'

'Look, if you've been posted to this...' Harry's words faltered as he glanced through the panoramic window at the crowded, rain-soaked streets of LP9, and the dingy, garish palaces providing its buildings. 'If you've been posted *here* as some kind of punishment gig, I understand.

I don't know, maybe you fouled up for good reasons. Maybe you were once an honest cop—'

Zalu jumped to his feet, shouting. 'Sergeant Xelos, get this alien out of here!'

'All I'm saying is that, if there was ever a time when you were a real cop – you know, someone who *didn't* neglect his duty – now's your chance to resurrect him.'

'*Sergeant Xelos!*'

'You won't regret it.'

'*Anybody!*' Zalu bellowed. '*Get this lunatic out of my office!*'

Two of the male officers appeared with punch-sticks, and began to hustle Harry.

'Once a cop, always a cop,' Harry said. 'Don't let anyone tell you different.'

The female officer now appeared.

'Xelos!' Zalu said. 'Where have you been?'

'You two, wait,' she said, stopping the arresting officers.

'Xelos, I asked you a question!' Zalu barked.

Unruffled, she turned to face him. 'Message for you, sir. From Central Despatch.'

'Put it through the appropriate channels.'

'It's for you personally, sir. From the Doctor.'

Zalu remained blank-faced, but Harry grinned as he looked from one to the other.

'Apparently,' she said, 'Xorg Krauzzen is holding a Torodon national against his will, with a view to liquidating him.' She clamped her mouth shut and waited.

'That's all there is?' Zalu asked.

'With all respect, sir, do we need any more?'

Zalu turned stiffly to the window, his hands knotted behind his back. Xelos nodded to the two other officers that Harry could be released.

They did as she said and backed from the room.

'Look…' Harry said, breaking the uncomfortable silence. 'I don't really know what's going on here. But I can tell good cops when I see them. And I reckon I'm in the presence of two right now.'

'Sergeant Xelos,' Zalu said slowly, 'are you A-listed for Operation Response?'

'I am, sir.'

'Be so good as to call one.'

'Yes, sir.' She clicked her heels before leaving.

Zalu glanced around at Harry. 'Am I to understand that you too are hoping to someday resurrect the good officer you once were?'

Harry straightened up. 'Very much so.'

'Then this is *your* chance too.'

Chapter
37

The TARDIS arrived on the viewing deck with its familiar fanfare of trumpet calls. And Amy bounced out of it with a fanfare of her own.

'I did it,' she shouted excitedly. 'I did it.'

Rory barely had a chance to compliment her on her 'retro Eighties' style, before she grabbed him and kissed him triumphantly.

'Sorry, no time for that,' the Doctor shouted, ushering forward a bunch of people she didn't know. They were bedraggled and sallow-faced. Two of them – a woman and teenage girl – hugged each other, weeping inconsolably. But the Doctor was impervious to such emotion. 'Into the TARDIS everyone, chop, chop!'

'But Doctor, I did it—' Amy began.

'Yes, well done. We can celebrate later. Who's this, by the way?'

Xorax had stepped out from the TARDIS and was staring around as if he couldn't quite believe that he wasn't still on board the *Ellipsis*.

'The prisoner I was telling you about,' she said.

'Good, good… Mr Xorax, you're extremely valuable to us.'

'I am?' Xorax replied, dazed.

'You are, and you'd be equally valuable dead, though I'm sure you wouldn't see it that way. So just step back inside the TARDIS.'

'How did… how did we get here?'

'Just do as I say.'

'I've got an even better idea!' came an echoing voice. 'Everyone do as *I* say, and you might live a few milliseconds longer!'

They whirled around.

About twenty metres from the tower, hovering silently, was a craft the Doctor knew could only be Zagardoz Xaaael's *Raptor-Bird*. It was built from gleaming black metal, and shaped like a falcon with its wings spread.

The voice, clearly that of Xaaael himself, spoke again: 'Nobody move, or I shall reduce this tower and everything on it to burning scrap, and that includes you, Doctor, and your precious machine.'

The Doctor glanced around. Only Xorax was near to the TARDIS, but he'd stepped outside and allowed its door to close, which meant it would need to be unlocked. The Doctor looked back at the *Raptor-Bird*. The double-barrels of two rapid-fire howitzers had emerged on the ridges of its wings. Even making a dash for it, no one would get into the TARDIS in time.

The other fugitives were frozen in place. Sophie and Dora had stopped sniffling, fear having overcome their sorrow.

A panel now slid open in the craft's hull, and a figure perambulated onto the starboard wing. It was Xaaael, clad in his exoskeleton of body armour. Two lesser gangsters followed him. All were armed with photon-rifles. An aluminium walkway extruded, pushing across the gulf between the craft and the tower. Xaaael sauntered across it almost casually. At the same time another figure swept up into view. It was no surprise to the Doctor to see Krauzzen himself, balanced expertly on his hover-plate. He too stepped onto the viewing deck, photon-rifle levelled. From the stairway below came grunts and clattering feet as his henchmen ascended by the tougher route.

A few seconds later, the viewing deck was crammed with personnel. The fugitives huddled together in the middle, hemmed in from all sides.

'Well, Doctor,' Krauzzen said. 'Run to ground at last. Though you've provided us with better sport than usual.'

'Don't kill that turncoat, Krauzzen!' someone shouted.

Krauzzen's men shifted aside to reveal Colonel Krelbin, flushed and sweating as he clambered over the safety barrier, his weapon slung on his broad back. He was soaked with sweat and his shoulders heaved, but his ice-blue stare was fixed on the Doctor with malign intensity.

The Doctor pursed his lips. 'Congratulations on surviving the shologgi, Colonel.'

'I didn't just survive it,' Krelbin snarled. 'I waited for it and ambushed it. Killed it bare-handed.'

'You're quite a man.'

'You won't talk your way out of this one.'

'Nor you, I fear,' the Doctor said. 'Wondering where your friends are yet?'

Krelbin looked puzzled, suddenly seeming to realise that no other members of the hunting party were present.

'Oh… try using your head,' the Doctor said. 'Krauzzen's finished on the Outer Rim. He's cleaning house before he leaves.'

Krelbin glanced distractedly from face to face, but perhaps it was Krauzzen and his men's chilling silence that made him snatch the weapon from his back and level it on the encircling crowd. 'Back off!' he shouted. 'All of you! You saw what this did to that Earthling on the roof over there!'

The Doctor gazed in fascination at the transmat-rifle that he'd thought lost.

'That's right, Doctor,' Krelbin sneered, retreating to the barrier. 'It's your own weapon. I found it while I was tracking you. It was hanging by its strap – too much of a risk for *you* to retrieve it, clearly, but no trouble for me. Now back off! That goes for you too, my lord! Are you so sure you want to side against me?'

'Well…' Krauzzen shrugged. 'Your tirades when you thought no one could hear *were* becoming a tad tiresome.'

'Hah! You want to hear me when I'm really angry. You know I'm not some playboy adventurer, Krauzzen! There isn't one of you here I'm not a match for…'

Krelbin choked on his final words.

He hadn't seen the figure glide up behind him on a hover-plate, pull the scalping-knife from its sheath, and jam it into his lower spine. He tottered forward, eyes goggling, blood frothing from his mouth. With his nervous system severed, his legs gave at the knees and he slumped down, falling hard onto his face.

His killer, Zarbotan, stepped awkwardly over the safety barrier.

He was in a gruesome condition. His clothes were charred tatters and much of his ectoderm, both real and synthetic, had melted away, revealing a cybernetic rib-work beneath, and a web of flexible plastic tubing, through which pumped his bodily fluids. Gelatinous organs pulsed inside plastic containers held by tensioned springs. Rotating sprockets and high tensile cord provided musculature.

Krauzzen raised an eyebrow. 'Better late than never, I suppose.'

'Forgive me, my lord,' Zarbotan replied. 'I got caught in the rain.'

Now that he no longer had a fleshy throat, his vocal cords, no more than a row of taut wires running vertically down into his chest cavity, visibly vibrated, creating an eerie, fluting echo. More than half his face was also missing, and a skullish steel mask was exposed. There was a low hum as his eyes irised to knife-points; he had focused through the crowd on Amy, who shrank back in horror.

'Well, isn't the party complete!' the Doctor said, clapping his hands. 'The hunters finally hook up with the hunted. Only this time it's the predators who've suffered the greater losses. Whatever happens next, I call that a result.'

Krauzzen pivoted to face him. 'You fascinate me,

Doctor. You've deceived me, betrayed me, humiliated me, you've cost me a significant income stream. And yet here you are, unafraid of my retaliation.'

The Doctor shrugged. 'Perhaps because I suspect you're the sort of materialistic rogue who usually looks to more lucrative solutions than mere vengeance.'

'You're right, of course. But that doesn't mean I don't take it. One good thing. Seeing as you're more interested in preserving life than ending it, I'm guessing the black-light explosive you've supposedly clamped to my vessel is… shall we say, pure imagination?'

'Do you want to take that chance?'

'There's no chance involved. Kill so many to save so few? That doesn't compute. *Xaaael!*' Krauzzen turned to his surly underling. 'I commend you for recapturing these creatures.' He pointed at Amy. 'Particularly this one.'

'It was nothing, my lord.'

'And was it also nothing to lose her in the first place?'

'My lord, I…'

'We'll talk about that later… but be assured, we *will* talk about it. In the meantime…' Krauzzen pointed at the TARDIS, 'how did that get down here when it was locked in my Secure Hold?'

'Teleportation,' Xaaael said. 'We tried to get a homing fix when it left the *Ellipsis*, but we lost the trace. I only looked down here because it seemed the obvious place.'

'Teleportation?' Krauzzen ran a gloved hand across the TARDIS's smooth panels. 'This must be a special device indeed?' He tried the door. 'Still locked, I see.'

'The girl has a key,' Zarbotan said.

Krauzzen turned to Amy, but the Doctor stepped between them.

'Even if Amy gives you her key, Krauzzen, it'll be no use to you. The secrets of the TARDIS are beyond your understanding. A lot of them are beyond mine, and I've flown her for centuries.'

'Why should we believe anything *you* say?' Zarbotan said, but Krauzzen held up a hand for silence.

'Tell me, Doctor… what exactly is this TARDIS?'

'A travel machine. The product of technology far, far in advance of your own. What you have here, my lord, is potentially the greatest asset in the galaxy.'

'Why do I sense you're about to try and make another deal with me?'

'Not a deal. A bet. You're a betting man, aren't you?'

'And this TARDIS is the prize?'

'The TARDIS and everything inside it.'

Krauzzen walked around the tall, blue box. 'Everything inside it isn't likely to be very much.'

'That's where you're wrong,' someone else said. It was Xorax, finally finding the courage to speak up.

'Kalik Xorax!' Krauzzen almost laughed. 'I thought I saw you skulking around.'

'I've been inside this TARDIS, my lord. It isn't just a spacecraft, it's a laboratory, an observatory, a repository of alien knowledge—'

'Shut up, Xorax!' Zarbotan growled. 'You have every reason to lie to us.'

'Would I lie about this, when you can so easily discover the truth?'

'Well, that's the trick, isn't it?' Krauzzen said, turning back to the Doctor. 'You want me to compete with you for this prize. Is that it?'

'And for the instruction manual,' the Doctor said. 'As I

say, you don't know how to operate the TARDIS.'

Krauzzen pondered. 'Why don't I just *force* you to show me?'

'Well, I suppose you could. I'd imagine you're very good at that sort of thing. But how will you ever be sure I'm giving you the full truth? For instance, you won't know if the first set of directional coordinates I calculate for you will lead to the innermost vault of the Central Bank of Torodon, or to the heart of a supernova.'

Krauzzen looked amused. 'And let me guess… if you win the bet, *you* will take the TARDIS, and everyone else is free to go?'

'It seems a small sacrifice on your part,' the Doctor said. 'You could gain an awful lot, and don't stand to lose much more than you've already lost.'

Krauzzen gave a crooked half-smile. 'You're obviously a man used to dictating terms, Doctor. Well… no longer. I'm not going to wager for property I already own.' He turned to his men. 'Take these prisoners to the *Ellipsis*. We can still make use of them. And this machine – we'll open it somehow. Doctor, much as I've enjoyed our acquaintanceship, I'm afraid you're too dangerous to be allowed to live.'

'Scared?' the Doctor asked.

'Kill him,' Krauzzen said, and half a dozen photon-rifles were raised.

The Doctor backed towards the safety barrier. 'Kill me if you want, but you men should remember this – Xorg Krauzzen is happy to watch others gamble, and to profit by it, but he doesn't have the nerve himself. Is a man like that fit to control your syndicate?'

'What do *you* think, Lord Xaaael?' Amy shouted.

'You've gambled countless times, yet the man who gives you orders hasn't got the guts!'

Xaaael said nothing, but regarded Krauzzen with open disdain. Several other gangsters noticed this, including Krauzzen.

'You have something to add, Xaaael?' Krauzzen asked.

'Not at all, my lord,' Xaaael replied, but his tone was contemptuous.

There was a long silence as the crime-lord glanced at his other followers' faces. Those with ambition or those he'd recently chastised returned his gaze boldly. Others found it difficult to look at him. Only Zarbotan made a point of standing by his side.

'It seems you're playing for more than just the TARDIS,' the Doctor said.

It perhaps wasn't unusual in the world of organised crime for syndicate leaders to be subtly challenged in this way. Doubtless it was common practice for the alpha-males in this society to occasionally need to enforce their leadership by proving themselves individually. But Krauzzen looked more than a little irritated.

'No one's asking the impossible, my lord,' the Doctor said. 'Just that you take my bet. And show your men your personal steel, no pun intended.'

Krauzzen rounded sharply on him. 'An astute move, Doctor. But understand – for this inconvenience, things may go all the harder for your friends.'

'I'm prepared to take that chance.'

'You didn't say what the bet was?'

The Doctor straightened the lapels of his jacket. 'I bet... I bet, Lord Krauzzen, that with a head start of just five minutes, I can make it all the way from this control tower, back across the industrial wastes of Gorgoror, to your Observation Booth. And that two of you – you yourself, and one other you nominate – will fail to prevent me.'

There was a brief silence, and then snickers from the watching gangsters.

'You realise those odds are ridiculously in my favour?' Krauzzen said.

'All the more reason for you to accept.'

'Doctor, this is suicide!' Rory shouted, but the Doctor put a finger to his lips.

Rory tried to shout again, but Amy clamped a hand to his mouth. She wore a grim smile, and kissed her husband on the cheek as if to reassure him that this was exactly the sort of ploy she'd expected the Doctor to try.

'You're quite serious about this?' Krauzzen said.

The Doctor offered his hand.

Krauzzen held back from shaking it. He knew it would make him appear nervous and unsporting, but all of a sudden there was something about this thin, oddly dressed individual, with his unruly hair and his pale, boyish face, that Krauzzen found menacing. The Doctor was articulate and intelligent; he had charm and wit – yet the very lack of threat he seemed to pose was in itself threatening. He hadn't just made it to the far end of the Gorgoror industrial complex, something never before achieved in the history of the fun hunts, but he'd also managed to bring most of the others with him. And he was unfazed by that achievement. He'd still had the energy and confidence to barter his way out of being executed.

The Doctor's bright eyes bored into Krauzzen as if

he'd expected nothing less than to create this doubt in his enemy. Still he offered his hand, but Krauzzen ignored it, pushing the Doctor aside and summoning Zarbotan to be his right-hand man.

'Weapons?' Zarbotan asked, slotting his hover-plate into the harness on his back.

'Only what we're carrying,' the Doctor said.

'You're carrying nothing.'

'And you're carrying a photonic arsenal. Even less reason for you to back out.'

'You can stop playing mind games,' Krauzzen retorted. 'There'll be no backing out. In fact, I'll even the odds. I'll give you more than five minutes. I'll give you ten.'

'You're too kind.'

'But know this.' Krauzzen now spoke in a low, intense monotone. 'When I've won, I'll be holding your friends as surety against you attempting to deceive me again. Even at the best of times it will be a living death for them, but it gets worse. You will give me full command of your TARDIS. You will tell me everything I need to know. *Everything!* You understand? If you fail to do that – on purpose, by accident, for any reason at all – these people will suffer unimaginable consequences! Am I clear?'

'Quite. Crystal. As mud.'

'Then we have our bet. The clock is ticking.'

The Doctor sprinted across the viewing deck, stripping his jacket en route. On reaching the barrier, he looped the garment over the zip-line, and leapt from the platform. 'Geronimo!' he shouted, rocketing over the chasm.

They flooded to the barrier to watch. When the Doctor was above the mountain of cinders, he dropped like a stone. Amy's heart was briefly in her mouth, as he plummeted a dozen metres – but landed relatively softly in the mass of yielding rubble, and rolled down its slope amid clouds of dust. Reaching the ground, he jumped to his feet, pulled his jacket back on, threw a salute towards the tower, and dashed off.

'Bet you didn't expect that?' Amy said to Krauzzen. 'That extra five minutes seems like a mistake now, eh?'

'Still smiling, I see,' Krauzzen replied. 'It suits you. I'll see to it that your mouth is surgically fixed that way.' He stalked off. 'Xaaael, take the TARDIS and these prisoners to the *Ellipsis*. And prep the ship to break orbit.'

Chapter
38

The first thing the Doctor did was try to get underground.

Krauzzen and Zarbotan would be coming after him on their hover-plates, which were capable of terrific speed. In the depthless maze of tunnels and conduits that was Gorgoror's underworld, this advantage would be reduced. But it was easier said than done. His nonchalant salute to the control tower might have implied that his fall into the cinders was all in a day's work, but it had knocked the wind from him. He stumbled groggily through several rows of derelict buildings, before hearing the distant throb of the *Raptor-Bird*'s engine.

He didn't pause to wonder what this meant, but clambered down a ladder into a manhole. Once a significant distance below the surface, he took a catwalk in the vague direction of the power plant. It was pitch-dark, so he used the light of his sonic screwdriver. Even so, he almost stepped over a precipice when he reached a point where the catwalk had simply rotted away. Sweat was soaking through his clothes as he doubled back. He was sure his ten-minute start was almost up already, and he hadn't put anything like enough distance between himself and his pursuers.

He took turns at random, running hard, though his feet were hammering on the old, rusty metal, and echoes rang throughout the subterranean grottos – something he couldn't afford for too long. He descended another ladder – only to find himself ankle-deep in cold, slopping water. He waded through this for fifty metres, stumbling on slimy sediment, until reaching a stone wall from which a culvert protruded. This was not much more than a metre in diameter, so he would only be able to move along it at a crouch. He heaved himself up into it and scrambled forward on hands and knees, now thinking he could hear voices behind him. No doubt he'd left a trail that a skilled tracker could follow, but it wasn't impossible that they'd have additional devices to hand – a heat-seeker or bio-tracer. A few metres later, the culvert sloped upward – and then began to spiral.

Even with two hearts pumping blood through a physiology superior in so many ways to a human's, the Doctor was now gasping for breath, barking his knees and elbows on rugged metal as he wormed his way around the twists and turns. The only consolation was that it would be equally difficult for Krauzzen and Zarbotan, though they, being at least semi-cybernetic, would tire even less quickly than he would. At the top of the spiral, he clambered over a concrete lip into a vast machine hall, though its towering stacks of equipment were little more now than oxidised frameworks of cogs and chains, and all of them sheathed with dust-webs.

He dashed across it towards another doorway, but almost halted when he glanced through one rusted mechanism, and saw floor space covered with what looked distinctly like human bones.

Even after everything he'd seen already, this was a gut-punching shock. There were many of them – far too many to have come from a mere handful of skeletons. Of course, whether the marrow had been sucked from these sad relics or they'd been incinerated by blaster fire was irrelevant. It all boiled down to the same thing now.

His anger gave him new energy. He ran on determinedly.

The next door led into a warehouse the size of a cathedral, and filled with steel barrels hoarded in great pyramids. The Doctor paused, panting. The barrels had been here untouched for so long that the green paint with which they'd been covered was flaking away, as were several bizarre markings stencilled on them in vivid red and resembling the upper portions of skulls. Almost certainly this was a warning regarding the contents of the barrels – they were toxic or flammable, or maybe both.

The Doctor again heard shouting voices. With nowhere else to go, he began to climb the nearest pyramid, but soon realised this was a mistake. It was tedious, agonising work, and as the barrels weren't fastened together, several slipped away beneath his feet, clattering to the floor. About twelve metres overhead, he saw what looked like the end of a conveyor system – steel struts with wheels along their sides – projecting from a hatchway. Only twelve metres, but the Doctor was so racked with fatigue it might as well have been a thousand. There came a shrill bleep behind him, and a photon blast hit the barrels below.

They exploded in a cloud of flame and glowing steel fragments.

The Doctor climbed as hard as he could. As the blazing barrels cascaded beneath him, others ignited. Balls of white-hot flame erupted into the air, and Xorg Krauzzen, riding his hover-plate with the honed skill of the Special Assault commando, swerved up between them. It was he who had fired the shot, and his photon-rifle was at his shoulder again.

The Doctor turned to face him. Krauzzen came to a halt a few metres away. His hair hung in a wild, unravelled mop. Despite his prosthetic features, he was grinning maniacally. 'The game's up, Doctor. I'd prefer you alive, but I'm sure your machine isn't so vital to me that dead won't be just as good.'

The Doctor didn't bother arguing, he just dived forward, catching hold of the hover-plate with his fingertips, his body swinging beneath it.

'You damn fool!' Krauzzen bellowed, as the plate tilted.

Desperately, he tried to rebalance himself, and set the vehicle in motion – swerving it up at ninety degrees to avoid the face of the pyramid. The Doctor clung on with both hands, but was whipped around like a piece of rag as the vehicle veered like a fighter plane, banking and hurtling across the massive chamber. Krauzzen was still struggling to regain control, and unintentionally crossed paths with Zarbotan, riding his own plate. Zarbotan jerked aside at so acute an angle that he was dismounted and went tumbling thirty metres to the warehouse floor, which he struck with a colossal impact. His hover-plate catapulted upward and vanished through the entrance to the conveyor, crashing and splintering as it caromed through the system's mechanical innards.

Krauzzen swore brutally, turned his rifle around and smashed down at the Doctor's fingers with its butt. First he aimed at the left hand, so the Doctor hung by the right. When Krauzzen aimed at the right, the Doctor swapped over.

'Damn you!' Krauzzen roared. 'You'll die for this! There's no bet, no deal... you'll just die!'

They'd now sailed out of the warehouse and were bulleting along a wide gangway bridged by numerous cross-girders. The first missed Krauzzen's head so closely that he was forced to duck. But now his rage turned to glee. He shifted position so that his plate rode downward. The Doctor saw the next cross-beam approach, realising that it would strike him full on. At the last second, he released his grip. He fell about four metres, bouncing and rolling on the straw-covered floor.

Bruised all over, he climbed to his feet and hobbled in the opposite direction – but only made it thirty metres before a nightmarish figure blocked his path.

It was Zarbotan, or what remained of him.

The hulking shape was not just mutilated by the acid, but was now broken as well: the steely mask of his face was crushed beyond recognition; one arm hung from its shoulder joint by a sparking wire; dark, oily fluids streamed from the rents where shattered mechanisms had pierced his plastic-coated organs; torn tubes and severed cables dangled between his legs. Despite this, Zarbotan lurched forward, whirring and clicking like a wind-up toy. The Doctor diverted sideways through an aperture and ran towards another vast, industrial building, though this was one he'd expected to see.

He glanced back. Zarbotan was still in pursuit, albeit far behind. However, high overhead, there was a shattering explosion as a streamlined shape burst from a crystal turret. It was Krauzzen, emerging like a bat from a belfry. With breathtaking skill, the diabolic figure performed a massive loop-the-loop, and came rocketing downward, his white mane streaming behind him. As he plummeted, he fired. The ground erupted in fury, but the Doctor ducked away from it, entering the next building and threading through a mass of fallen timbers and masonry. Beyond this, he attempted to descend a switchback stair, the well of which was equally crammed with wreckage. Tripping, he fell full-length down a perilous gradient, which only terminated when he crashed through a glass partition, and found himself on the lip of a gargantuan crater.

He peered down. As he'd hoped – a concrete podium was visible about three metres below, overhanging the abyss. He lowered himself towards it, only for a shape to whistle past, narrowly missing his head. Dropping the rest of the way, the Doctor landed awkwardly, twisting his ankle and knocking the wind from himself for the second time in the last few minutes.

He could only lie there, sobbing for breath. The gaping aperture where he and Dora had blown the door down earlier was still open, but suddenly he was too wearied to move. He tried to get up, but slumped down again onto his side.

Krauzzen arced around in the vast space above the crater, before racing back down until he was on the same level as his prey, whereupon he slowed to a hover.

'A good chase, Doctor. But your success has been your

undoing.' He levelled his photon-rifle. 'I now know for a fact that I could never relax if you were still alive.'

Before he could trigger the weapon, it flipped from his hands and vanished into the gulf below. He looked baffled rather than angry – a bafflement which turned swiftly to panic as he slowly began to descend. His feet slipped as he struggled to maintain balance on a hover-plate which, despite his best efforts, was turning upright.

'Problem, my lord?' the Doctor wondered. 'Feeling the weight of your sins?'

With a strangled cry, Krauzzen dived from his steel plate, which nose-dived into the darkness below. He caught a jutting fragment of timber, and hung there.

After contorting into a fiendish grin a few seconds earlier, his normally expressionless face now contorted with agony. Of course, he wasn't just hanging on for his life; suddenly he was having to resist an irresistible force.

The Doctor got up and dusted himself, though the sonic screwdriver in his jacket pocket was tugging so hard that he had to brace his legs apart to keep his stability.

'You'll notice, how every bit of metal round here is warping downward into this crater,' the Doctor said. 'That's what's happening to the metal components filling your body. This wasn't what I wanted, but in the end you gave me no choice.'

'Blast you!' Krauzzen hissed, glutinous yellow sludge foaming from his mouth.

'It's a kind of solace, Krauzzen, to know that there's at least one power out here – even if it's only the magnetic core of a nuclear reactor – to which you are answerable.'

Krauzzen could no longer speak. His body had

noticeably elongated.

As the Doctor watched, his clothing ripping asunder, and then, beneath that, the flesh parted as his joints cracked and a rain of blood burst forth. There was a series of sickening crunches as gears and sprockets tore loose from moorings, as circuitry was rent from its boarding and sliced through organ and artery. Krauzzen mouthed a final silent scream, before dropping into the blackness, a distorted, dismembered relic.

All that remained was his left hand – completely organic, but with only a torn stump where its wrist should be, clutching a knot of timber. A testimony, the Doctor supposed, to the physical strength of the flesh and blood creature Krauzzen once had been. He kicked out, and the hand fell from sight.

Wearily, he backed across the platform and moved through the blown-open doorway, where he was thankful to be free of the magnetic field. His sonic screwdriver relented in its efforts to escape, and he was able to straighten himself, and mop back his sweaty hair. He set off walking – only to find Zarbotan in his path.

The Doctor froze. For an absurd moment he raised his fists, a pint-sized pugilist.

But Zarbotan didn't respond. In fact, he didn't move at all.

He'd loomed out of the gloom like some great chunk of industrial sculpture. The last vestige of his flesh had been sloughed away, and those few fleshy organs inside him had ceased to function. He was no longer a living thing; just the shell of one.

There was no life in his metallic eyes.

Cautiously, the Doctor stepped to one side of him and

around to the back. He circled the giant several times, before pushing him, and watching him topple forward and strike the ground with a hollow clang.

Chapter
39

The Raptor-Bird was in the process of docking with the *Ellipsis*, but on board it every eye, those of captives and captors alike, were fixed on its main screen. They'd just watched Krauzzen meet his fate, and were now staring wide-eyed at a grainy picture of the inert junk that had once been known as Zarbotan.

From his command chair, Xaaael regarded the image with amazed fascination.

'There!' Amy said triumphantly. She and the other prisoners stood behind him, still under the rifles of his henchmen. 'You have to release us. That was the deal.'

Xaaael rose slowly to his feet. 'Any deal the Doctor made with Lord Krauzzen died with Lord Krauzzen. The *Ellipsis* is now mine. Along with everything and everyone on board.'

'You're a liar and a cheat!' Amy shouted.

'Finally she understands how we make our living,' he said.

'The Doctor will come after us again.'

'Not without his TARDIS.' A vibration passed through the craft as they connected with the *Ellipsis*. 'Get them aboard. Put them back in the holding cells.'

With much growling and pushing, the prisoners were herded into an airlock. Beyond this lay another passage made from billowing fabric. They tumbled down it, prisoners and gangsters together. Amy was last, and hung back. One of the gangsters hung back as well. It was Zalizta. He regarded Xaaael with deep scepticism.

'You have a problem with me, Zalizta?' Xaaael asked.

'This takeover should be put to the syndicate,' Zalizta replied. 'It should be voted on.'

Xaaael's lips tightened until they were livid white lines, but he nodded. 'I understand that. And we *will* vote. But later. For now I'm assuming emergency command. Agreed?'

Zalizta still seemed unsure.

'Now do as I say, and put her aboard.'

Reluctantly, Zalizta turned to Amy and grabbed her by the scuff of the neck – and was promptly shot in the back by Xaaael's photon-pistol. The blast hurled him clean across the airlock, fusing him into its far bulkhead.

Amy gazed at Xaaael, stunned.

He levelled his pistol at her. 'And I thought *you* people were slow on the uptake.'

With no choice, she allowed him to usher her along the gravity-free gangway.

'I'll tell your men what you've just done,' she said over her shoulder.

'You think they'll care once they get their hands on the plunder I'll secure with your teleportation machine?'

'You are evil.'

Xaaael laughed. 'There's no such thing as evil on the Outer Rim. Just "winner takes all".'

They alighted together in the *Ellipsis* airlock, which slammed behind them.

'That means I take everything,' Xaaael said. 'This mothership, its crew, full control, full power, full responsibility for what was once called "the Krauzzen Syndicate".'

'Excellent news, Xaaael,' a bass voice declared, as the muzzle of a photon-pistol was pressed into his right temple. 'On the basis of which confession, I am arresting you for kidnapping and conspiring to murder Kalik Xorax.'

Xaaael was too stunned to respond. He watched dully as his own weapon was wrested from his grasp.

His captives now stood to one side, rubbing at their hurts, while all across the boarding area police officers in combat armour had their guns drawn. Most of his own men were already handcuffed and lying on the floor. Others were in the process of being cuffed. Xaaael glanced sideways – into a face that criminals of his ilk had once feared, and perhaps would learn to do so again: Kobal Zalu.

'We can do this the easy way,' Zalu said, digging the muzzle of his weapon into the back of Xaaael's neck and forcing him across the deck to join his comrades. 'Or we can do it the hard way. Something inside me hopes you opt for the latter.'

Xaaael still couldn't quite believe what had happened. Through a viewing port he was astounded to see dozens of police cruisers in position around the *Ellipsis*. He and his men had been so busy watching the events on Gorgoror, they hadn't noticed them as they'd approached.

'Are you mad?' he stuttered. 'You know you can't do this!'

'Can't I?' Zalu holstered his weapon, and clapped one hand on the shoulder of Kalik Xorax, who treated Xaaael to a reptilian smile. 'We have all the evidence we need right here. And before you say anything else, Xorax is about to disappear into a witness protection programme. So you and all your powerful political friends – assuming you have any left now Krauzzen has gone – will never hear from him again until he's testifying against you in court.'

'Xorax, you traitor!' Xaaael spat, as his hands were twisted behind his back. 'You were one of us! You swore an oath to Lord Krauzzen!'

Xorax shrugged. 'Any oath I swore to Lord Krauzzen… died with Lord Krauzzen.'

Xaaael choked to hear his own weasel words used against him.

'Take him away!' Zalu roared. 'Take them all!'

With much shouting, the mobsters were removed from the boarding area. Zalu turned towards the human prisoners, who still huddled together uncertainly.

'You people must have put up quite a battle to have survived,' he said. 'I'm sorry we didn't get here sooner. Did you incur many losses?'

Amy glanced at Sophie and Dora. Their eyes were still red-rimmed, still downcast.

'Just one,' Rory said stepping forward. 'This is his family.'

Zalu regarded the women sympathetically.

'I'll miss him too,' Rory added. 'Harry was one of the best.'

Zalu's expression changed. 'Harry… Mossop?'

Rory was surprised. 'You knew him?'

'An ex-policeman,' Zalu said, 'who, even if he wasn't armed, could probably talk a criminal gang into submission? In fact, he could talk *anyone* into submission?'

Rory and the Mossop girls glanced at each other, mystified.

'Wouldn't you say that was true?' Zalu asked them.

'It's very true,' Dora replied, 'but I don't understand…'

Zalu pointed along a connecting companionway.

Rory wasn't sure whether he or the two women were the most stunned to see who was now coming along it, dressed in Torodon police armour and in company with a tall female officer.

'Bridge secured, Chief,' Harry said, throwing up a salute.

Dora and Sophie screamed in unison.

They hared across the boarding area together and leapt onto Harry, who almost collapsed beneath their combined weight and his own bellowing laughter. Only with difficulty did he manage to explain about the transportation device the Doctor had disguised as a deadly weapon.

Amy gave Rory a knowing wink.

'Hello on the *Ellipsis*!' came a familiar voice. 'More to the point, I suspect… hello Kobal Zalu!'

They moved into an adjoining security cell, where a bank of monitors gave various views of the Gorgoror surface. One of these portrayed the viewing deck at the top of the control tower, where the Doctor stood looking up at them.

'Can anyone hear me?' he called.

Sergeant Xelos made contact with the Bridge, and the ship's computer patched them through to the surface.

'Hello Doctor,' Zalu replied. 'Good to see you've survived. Again.'

'Ah, Zalu. I was hoping you'd get around to doing your job at some point.'

'I've only half done it. Obtaining convictions on this space rabble will be a sight more difficult than arresting them.'

'If anyone can do it, Zalu, you're the man. Is everybody else safe and sound?'

'We are, Doctor,' Dora shouted. 'Thank you so much. We owe you everything.'

'Well…' The Doctor shrugged. 'Actually you owe it to your husband. I provided Zalu with the necessary legality to intercede on your behalf. But I suspect it was Harry who applied most of the pressure.'

Dora hugged her husband all the harder.

Harry smiled at Zalu. 'I didn't have to apply too much.'

'I'll send a shuttle down to pick you up,' Zalu said.

'No need. Amy flew the TARDIS before. I'm sure she can do it again. You all right with that, Amy? Same as last time?'

'After what we've been through, it'll be a doddle,' Amy replied.

'Just don't forget your passengers. We've a few people to take home.'

Chapter
40

When the TARDIS materialised on the control tower, the Doctor was standing by the safety barrier. Amy went out to him first.

'Well!' she said, striking a pose made all the more dramatic by her snazzy retro outfit. 'We did it!'

'Yes, we did,' he replied, though for some reason he wasn't quite as euphoric as she'd expected.

The others now spilled from the TARDIS. Rory, who looked worn out by his exertions, stood back while the one-time prisoners flocked to their saviour, so glad they'd been rescued that they barely mentioned the anomaly of having travelled in a craft that was bigger inside than outside. One by one, they pumped the Doctor's hand. In Dora and Sophie's case, they hugged him and kissed him on the cheeks.

Harry came last; he looked as tired as Rory, but seemed a little more relaxed. He was still wearing the police armour.

'Suits you,' the Doctor commented.

'Chief Zalu offered me a job,' Harry said.

'Wow!'

'As a fully fledged LP9 cop.' Harry shrugged. 'I was tempted. Very. But Earth is our home... Things are pretty rough down there at present, but now the Mossops are back together, I reckon we can tackle anything.' He spoke with strength and confidence. His wife and daughter stood one to either side, their arms around him. 'When we're solid like this, we fear nothing.'

'Excellent,' the Doctor replied. 'That's how it should be.'

'The first thing we're doing is going on holiday,' Dora said. 'Just a cheap package deal. So we can get reacquainted.'

The family laughed together as she led them back to the TARDIS.

'I wouldn't mind going on holiday,' the Doctor murmured. 'Holidays are cool.'

The other passengers now filed into the TARDIS as well. Eventually, only the Doctor, Amy and Rory remained on the deck.

The Doctor smiled, though again it lacked triumphalism. 'Rory, we've got plenty of room. Do you want to get them all settled? So they're not fiddling with things they shouldn't.'

For once too tired to be worried about leaving the Doctor and Amy alone, Rory nodded and stepped back inside. When he'd gone, the Doctor turned to the barrier. The ruined landscape below was silent and empty.

Sensing what the problem was, Amy went and stood beside him.

'I wonder how many have died here?' she said. 'In total.'

'Oh… too many.'

'We could go back and save more of them.'

The Doctor sighed. 'Same old conundrum, Amy.'

'But we *could*?'

'Yes, we could.' He glanced round at her. 'But I'll be honest with you. I'm not sure I want to go back to a time when Xorg Krauzzen is still alive. Meeting him once was quite enough for me. Now, why don't you go and get changed, eh? That punk rock thing… seems a bit old hat.'

She nodded and smiled – and went back into the TARDIS.

The Doctor peered again at the surface of Gorgoror, and remembered the scattered bones he'd seen in its old machine hall.

He never liked thinking about the endless possibilities his ability to travel in time created. So mostly, he didn't. But sometimes – as now – it wasn't easy. In a minute, he'd go back inside the TARDIS, hit the dematerialisation control and watch through the console monitor as this hellish wasteland faded into static.

If only he could do that with the thoughts inside his head.